Ice-cool superwoman—that was Sister
Slater of Women's Surgical Ward. It took
the new heart and lung consultant Giles
Levete, with his mocking comments
and laughing eyes, to prove that she
was human after all. And in uncovering
her secret life he found they had the
most surprising circumstances in
common . . .

Holly North was born in Cambridge in 1955. She read History at Durham University and in 1978 married her American husband, Sam. His career has taken them all over the world, from New York and Paris to Saudi Arabia and, at the moment, Japan. Holly teaches English and restores oriental carpets when she can—and when she can't, she keeps herself sane by writing about her home country. She's a passionate advocate of the NHS, which looks all the more impressive from abroad, and consults her brother-in-law, who is a paediatrician, for much of the medical detail in her books.

SISTER SLATER'S SECRET

BY
HOLLY NORTH

MILLS & BOON LIMITED

15–16 BROOK'S MEWS
LONDON W1A 1DR

First published in Great Britain 1986 by Mills & Boon Limited

© Holly North 1986

Australian copyright 1986 Philippine copyright 1986

ISBN 0 263 75425 1

Set in 11 on 11½ pt Linotron Times
03–0686–50,000

Photoset by Rowland Phototypesetting Limited Bury St Edmunds, Suffolk Printed and bound in Great Britain by Collins, Glasgow

CHAPTER ONE

'I WOULDN'T say that she's a complete martinet . . .' Leaning heavily on his cane, Barney Morton, general surgeon at Highstead Hospital, limped down the corridor in the direction of the surgical wards. He'd been off his crutches for a week now, after a month confined to bed, and was getting back into something nearer his stride. At his side Giles Levete, the new cardiologist, wondered what Barney had done to sustain such an injury. His brief explanation about an abandoned skateboard and a steep rockery path had seemed too bizarre to be true.

'We'll find her on Women's Surgical,' Barney said cheerfully, hobbling around a badly parked trolley. 'She's a good ally to have, Giles. A first-class nurse, runs her ward as if it were a platoon in the army. So you'll have to forgive any of her little foibles for the sake of your patients.'

'She sounds perfectly awful,' Giles shuddered. 'One of the old school, I suppose. I hope she's going to retire soon?'

'In twenty-five years' time, perhaps,' Barney laughed. 'Meanwhile, she's just what we need for the surgical ward. Fastidious, intelligent and with that sixth sense that tells her when something's going to blow. If she's a bit standoffish that's a small price to have to pay. Just don't go hanging around there wasting time, that's all.'

'I assure you I'll avoid her like the plague!' Giles

threw back his leonine head and gave a throaty laugh. 'I don't expect to have many patients for her ward, not in the first few months, anyway. Does she have much experience of heart and lung work?'

'Plenty. I doubt very much if you'll catch Sister Slater napping—which is something you'll learn to be grateful for, I tell you.' They walked on, Giles measuring his pace to suit Barney's faltering steps, feeling a little foolish at the mincing stride he was forced to affect. His long legs weren't made for such a slow pace.

'I hear you've just lost your junior registrar,' he ventured urbanely, having heard something of the sort in the dining-room during lunch.

'Not lost her completely,' Barney grimaced. 'She'll be around—she's transferred to the new unit, the plastic surgery and burns unit.'

'I've read all about it,' Giles murmured, intrigued. 'It's a feather in her cap, I imagine. She must have been good—and you must be put out at losing her.'

'She had to marry the man in charge to get the transfer,' his companion said darkly. 'Though I dare say they'll be happy enough; and I dare say he's just the sort a nice young woman like that would go for.'

Giles smiled at the barely concealed resentment in Barney's voice. He didn't envy the poor girl having to slave away under Barney's direction, and from what he'd heard, Nick Da Costa was tall, dark, handsome and quite unfairly brilliant when it came down to reconstructive surgery. Who could blame her for falling in love? He allowed a breath to hiss between his teeth. Love was not an emotion he was going to indulge in ever again. It had brought him enough trouble, heaped coals upon his head, brought about this change in his circumstances. Perhaps Mrs Da Costa was going to get more than *she'd* bargained for, too.

He turned into the entrance of Women's Surgical and followed Barney through the swing doors. A neat figure in the blue and white uniform of the hospital dashed across their path and into an office. Giles was aware merely of sleek dark hair pinned neatly under the hat and an elegant economy of movement as she swept through his field of vision.

'Ah, that's Sister now!' Barney exclaimed, and he lead the way into her room. 'Sister, let me introduce—'

But he got no further, for Louise Slater looked up calmly and said in her cool voice, 'I'm afraid you'll have to wait just a moment, Mr Morton. I have to attend to a patient.' And she had disappeared from view, out into the ward, as her final word reached their ears.

'Sister Slater, the human whirlwind—I know the type,' Giles murmured to Barney. 'A place for everything and everything in its place—and that goes for consultant surgeons, too.'

Barney stood apologetic, slightly chastened. 'It's operating day,' he explained.

'Right, Nurse Rees, let's get Mrs Elsdon back into the oxygen tent.' Louise bit back the angry words that queued in her throat to be voiced; anger with Jenny Rees, the young staff nurse whose arrival on the ward three weeks ago had resulted in chaos, and anger with Mr Morton, who should have known better than to bring a visitor to the ward on the main operating day of the week.

'It's all right, Mrs Elsdon, you'll soon feel better. Just hold the mask to your face while we get you back into bed.' With practised skill, Louise went to lift the patient—but Jenny failed to raise her at the same moment and all the weight was left for Sister to bear. Feeling her bones creak, Louise made a superhuman effort and hoisted Mrs Elsdon, who was scarcely sylph-like, into position. Eyes carefully cast down, Jenny hastened to pull the tent over the upper part of the bed and Louise switched the oxygen cylinder full on, feeling her strained back pulling with every move she made. She signalled to Mrs Elsdon to remove the mask and peered through the plastic barrier to have a look at her colour.

'She's much better,' Jenny Rees declared. 'She was very cyanosed when I spotted her.'

With the patient unable to hear from within the tent, Louise said quietly, 'But the whole point of the matter, Staff Nurse, is that I specifically asked you to keep an eye on her while she was out of bed, and you didn't do it.' She tried to straighten, but an agonising twinge warned her that it would be better to remain at this uncharacteristic angle.

'Furthermore, Staff Nurse,' she muttered through gritted teeth, 'I warn you I am quite indestructible. I survived walking into the trolley you left outside my office door yesterday, and I survived the electric shock I got after you'd managed to short-circuit the autoclave, so dropping Mrs Elsdon on me is unlikely to make any difference.'

'I'm terribly sorry, Sister, I didn't mean to—'

'I know you didn't mean to, Nurse,' Louise said, sorry now for her petty outburst. She was rewarded by a shy glance for reassurance from the gangling new girl. 'Perhaps you would go along to the office now and ask Mr Morton if he'll come and have a quick check of Mrs Elsdon's breathing. And when you've done that, relieve Staff Nurse Simpson.'

'Yes, Sister.'

'And don't run!' Louise had to warn her as she set off at the kind of pace that would have had Sebastian Coe looking to his laurels.

Mrs Elsdon, banked with pillows, moaned and began to cough miserably. She gestured that she wanted to lie down.

'No, my dear, you *must* sit up. I'm sorry that it's so uncomfortable, but really, it does help your breathing. Pull yourself into position, Mrs Elsdon.'

Weakly, the patient did as she was told, Louise assisting her as much as she could with her back creaking as if it would break. Indestructible indeed! With Jenny Rees around, she was going to have to eat her words one of these days.

'Here's the cup.' Louise reached into the tent, removed the mask, and handed Mrs Elsdon the covered sputum cup into which she had to cough the discharge that had invaded her lungs. Bronchiectasis was a nasty disease, not only for the patient, but for the surrounding family, colleagues and friends of the sufferer, whose appalling breath and constant coughing were enough to annoy anyone. It was hardly, Louise reminded her nurses nearly every day when they complained, Mrs Elsdon's fault that she had contracted such an anti-social disease.

When Mrs Elsdon had finished coughing and had handed back the container, Louise took her pulse and blood pressure. Both were a little higher than they should be—higher than they had been two hours ago, when they had last been checked, she noted, surveying the chart at the end of the bed.

'I think I've pulled the stitches,' Mrs Elsdon complained, touching her chest gingerly.

Louise was alert. Mrs Elsdon had had a pleural drain inserted in her chest wall to take away any excess fluid that built up after the operation to remove the infected part of her right lung. It had been taken out a few days ago and carefully stitched so that no air could get inside. Should that stitch have gone, her lung might collapse again. And a collapsed lung would show itself in shortness of breath, discomfort, heightened heart rate . . .

'Do you have a problem, Sister?' Giles Levete was at her side before she had even heard him arrive.

'Thank you,' Louise replied almost automatically, 'but I think Mr Morton will be able to deal with it.' Who was this tall, slightly scruffy man?

'Mr Morton is still only half-way down the ward.' He gestured back to where Barney was hobbling along with cheerful, overweight Rosemary Simpson at his elbow. 'And I'm Giles Levete, the new heart and lung specialist. From what I see here, you need my services . . .'

He allowed the final words to trail off with the slightest suggestive hint that Louise tried to ignore; as she tried to ignore the stabbing pain that suddenly distracted her. 'Well . . .' She supposed he must be who he said he was.

'Mrs Elsdon's a bronchiectasis case. She had a right lobectomy eight days ago and was allowed out of bed for the first time today. My staff nurse has just found her cyanosed and short of breath, and

I'm a little worried that she has air in the pleural cavity. Would you be willing to check it for me? Her surgeon is probably still in theatre.'

'Of course.' He was suddenly serious, turning immediately to wash his hands at the sink by the patient's bed while Louise drew the curtains.

Staff Nurse Simpson and Mr Morton arrived at that point, having enjoyed a good joke on the way. 'The dressings trolley, please, Nurse,' Louise commanded, chagrined to find her dependable fourteen stone junior in gales of laughter when *she* could barely move, so bad was the pain in her back.

'Do you need me, Sister, or have you got Mr Levete down to work already?' Barney asked politely.

'Everything is under control, thank you, Mr Morton. Why don't you go back to the office and sit down?'

'Push off, Barney. If I have to go to theatre with this I don't want you hanging around.' Giles Levete's deep, musical voice pierced the bed-curtains.

'I'm obviously not wanted,' Barney said with mock hurt in his voice, and followed Rosemary Simpson's broad beam back the way they had come.

Pale-faced as another wave of pain overtook her, Louise re-entered Mrs Elsdon's cubicle, to find Mr Levete already confidently introducing himself to his patient, who was looking up at him with trusting wonder.

For there was something about Giles Levete that inspired confidence. It couldn't be his appearance, Louise thought critically, for he didn't look much like a hospital consultant. He was very, very tall, and rangy with it, as if he'd lost a lot of weight recently. His hair, an attractive dark blond that many a woman might have envied, lay in curls all over his head and fell too long at the back. It was the kind of head Louise had seen on Roman coins, with a strong nose and sensual, well-defined lips, like those famous emperors who'd had thoroughly unsavoury lifestyles.

Giles Levete probably didn't live a very savoury life either, Louise decided, helping him to place the oxygen mask over Mrs Elsdon's face, remove the tent, and then lift her nightgown. He had bags under his heavy-lidded eyes, those eyes too quick to show amusement, and a confident air that suggested he was getting plenty of what he liked —which probably explained his thinness, she decided. He was like a sleepy, worn-out lion—a lion who could definitely do with a trim. And a dry-clean, too, for he had a spot of something, gravy perhaps, on his left lapel, and his suit, though once, she felt, very good, had reached the end of its useful life about a year ago. It wasn't embarrassingly awful, just slightly sheeny, and with a thread beginning to show at the cuff.

Nurse Simpson arrived with the trolley. 'Thank you. Leave it here.'

'Very well, Sister.'

The gleam of a smile lit Giles Levete's face. It had been a long time since he'd heard such military talk on a hospital ward. Sister Slater obviously ran the sort of tight ship that nurses either loved or hated. And why *was* she holding herself so stiffly, with her lips clenched tightly together as if she might scream as she moved?

He watched her move almost gingerly to the basin and wash her own hands again. She was a trim woman, not much over thirty, he guessed. She had fine, soft dark hair, pinned back—too neatly, he thought—and strong, clean bone structure. Nice legs, too, if only she'd walk properly, he thought appreciatively. Pity she was one of these dragon Sisters, unmarried, hide-bound by the book, too up-tight to really enjoy life. Look at her now, bending to reach the towel as if she'd break . . .

They gently removed the dressing from Mrs Elsdon's chest, Louise holding the kidney bowl to receive the soiled gauze and steadfastly refusing to look him in the eye. Giles was amused and made her reach out to accept the last layer of tulle. He saw her cheeks blanch and heard the slight gasp that went through her as a spasm of cutting pain sliced through her poor, strained back. For a moment she closed her eyes.

'Sister, are you all right?' He sounded suddenly concerned and she looked up into the stunning blue depths of his eyes and felt frightened by their fascination.

'I've strained my back,' she admitted. Better to let him know than have him wondering what kind of an idiot she was, moving as if she was on castors, she decided.

'Shall I call a nurse?' he asked.

'No, it's not that bad,' she breathed, 'let's continue.' And continue they did.

'It's fine. No infection, no air.'

'That's good, is it?' Mrs Elsdon piped up.

'Yes, very good. You didn't actually want to go back to theatre, did you, Mrs Elsdon?' Giles asked candidly, and Louise's disapproval of such levity showed in her eyes.

'Perhaps you ought to be a bit more upright, though,' he suggested coolly. 'And we'll have you leaning slightly over to the left so that the scar tissue is slightly stretched—both on the surface and in your lungs. That way you'll retain as much movement and expansion as possible.'

Her stone-walling technique had got through to him, she could tell by his raised eyebrow and tightened lips. Well, she didn't care what he thought of her; she didn't approve of over-familiar surgeons, and that was that. Give her someone like Miss Meredith—or Mrs Da Costa as she now was. Her combination of reserve and quiet confidence were ideal.

'Mrs Elsdon's on antibiotics?' Mr Levete asked casually, going again to the basin in the ritual of absolute hygiene that became second nature after fifteen years of surgery.

'Yes.' Louise named the drug and the dosage without having to refer to the chart at the end of the bed. Irritatingly, Giles was impressed. Few ward sisters, beset as they were with reams of paperwork and committees as well as nursing supervision, knew the details of their patients' drugs. But of course, Sister Slater would . . .

'And I presume that she's already receiving inhalations?' Giles could have kicked himself. With his mind on those fascinating, clear blue eyes of hers, he'd fallen into her hands. For on a ward like this, treatment would be absolutely by the book; *of course* the patient would be taking benzoin inhalations to speed up the expulsion of the infected sputum.

'Thrice daily.' Louise Slater's voice held more than a hint of scathing disbelief that he could doubt her competence.

'Well then, Sister,' Mr Levete drawled deliberately, mocking her precision, 'at the moment there's nothing more I can suggest. Get her own surgeon to take a look at her at his convenience, and until then, get your troops . . . sorry, your nurses, to keep a watch over her.'

'Very well. Thank you, Mr Levete. I'll take the dressings trolley back to its proper place,' she said stiffly, having noted his slip of the tongue—or was it deliberate?

'Oh no, you don't, Sister.' Giles Levete shot out a long-fingered hand and stayed her. 'I'd like to take a look at your back before you go doing anything else.' A twinkle of mischief glowed in his eye at this bright idea. Perhaps he could give the poor, put-upon nurses of the ward something to chuckle about as they went about their daily grind under the orders of this Genghis Khan. 'To your office—carefully!' he commanded, and guiding her by the elbow, forced Louise up the ward.

'This really isn't necessary . . .' she protested as he opened the door and swept her in, but he wasn't listening.

'Nurse!' SRN Halliday and Joan Watson, auxiliary, both came at a trot from the nurses' station, where they had been monitoring the progress of the eleven patients who'd just come up from Recovery after surgery. 'Tea and codeine for Sister, please, Nurses—but give us ten minutes first.' He bestowed a charming smile on their bemused faces and waved off Joan Watson's troubled, 'What on earth's happened to Sister?'

For the truth of the matter was that although
Louise had the reputation for being a bit of a slave
driver, and although it was widely rumoured that
she had iced water in her veins instead of blood,
Women's Surgical, working under Sister Slater,
was where every ambitious and competent nurse in
the hospital would like to be. Sister Slater was as
efficient as every staff nurse would like to be. Sister
Slater was utterly unflappable in a crisis and gave
her staff and patients the confidence to do the kind
of things they'd otherwise never have dared to do.
Sister Slater had the personal discipline to remember to call you 'Nurse' in front of the medical staff,
reminding them of your status and qualifications,
and by your first name in the sluice or the office. If
you survived a year or two under her regime, you
could pride yourself on being a good nurse. And
that was why even Jenny Rees, disaster-prone as
she was, felt grimly determined to stick it out—for
she knew that if she was going to be a good nurse,
this was her opportunity to learn how to become one.

'Now, I want you to lean over the desk, hands
there . . .' he instructed.

'Really, Mr Levete, this is quite ridiculous! I've
just strained my back, that's all. A couple of pain-
killers now and a hot bath later—'

'And you'll be in agony for another week,' he
finished succinctly. 'Take off your belt, Sister, and
lean over as far as you can go.' He bent her over
the desk; it was painful, and Louise decided that
obedience was likely to be less uncomfortable than
resistance. 'That's far enough. I'm just going to
check your vertebrae.'

At least he hadn't asked her to take her uniform
off, Louise consoled herself as she supported her-

self on the desk. This was so humiliating! Hadn't she always emphasised to her staff that they should be careful when lifting a patient to avoid such a back strain as this?

'Ooooh!' She tried to bite back the exclamation, but failed.

'Sorry, Sister—did that hurt?' Despite his half-amused tone, Giles felt himself strangely moved by Louise's slim waist under his long fingers. She was really quite a small woman, he realised. It was something about her uniform and manner that gave the impression she was bigger and tougher than she actually was. He was deliberately more careful as he moved on down her back to the lumbar region and felt her stiffen to his touch. She must be in pain, quite bad pain.

For a moment she turned her head to try to see what he was doing, aware of a warmth beginning, despite the pain, to seep into her limbs; a warmth she had consciously decided she could not afford to permit herself again some fifteen years ago; a warmth she thought she had forgotten about. And then his fingers probed, and she winced.

Above her, Giles caught the pained expression. 'It's all right . . . all right,' he said gently, as if he was soothing a child. 'Just a moment more, Sister. Try to relax—I know it must hurt.' And this time there was no mocking undertone, just a reassuring murmur and the feel of his hands, so gentle, so firm, as they teased their way down her spine . . .

They stood there for a moment when he had finished, his hands resting lightly on the curve of her hip, where her body flared gently out from its neat waist, neither of them daring to move or talk. For somewhere along the line, chemistry had

begun to take over from detached medical judgment, and although everything had remained perfectly above board and ethical, both were stiflingly
aware of all that had happened.

It was Staff Nurse Halliday who broke the atmosphere, for she knocked briskly on the door and then
entered bearing her tray of tea, only to be brought
up short by the sight of Sister bent over her desk
and this new consultant standing over her in a
highly compromising position.

'Sister!'

Startled, Louise straightened briskly and felt Mr
Levete's hands drop from her. She grimaced as the
pain caught her off guard again. 'Just my back,
Staff. Mr Levete was checking to see I hadn't
impacted a disc.'

'I see, Sister.' Carolyn Halliday invested the
word with a wealth of meaning. 'I've brought
codeine, Sister. And there's tea for you both.'

'Sister really ought to go home, Nurse. Would
you be able to cope if she did?' Giles Levete
reached nonchalantly across the desk and picked
up the prescription pad from his briefcase, which
he'd left in the office when Nurse Rees had
appeared to ask for help with Mrs Elsdon.

'Yes, I think so, sir,' Carolyn replied.

'There's really no need to call me sir,' Giles
murmured as he scribbled flamboyantly on the pad.
'I'm Mr Levete, the new heart and lung consultant
—and I can't abide stuffy formality. It stops things
getting done, in my opinion.'

'On the contrary, it's the only way to get things
done,' Louise interrupted. 'If we all spent our time
making small talk the hospital would grind to a halt.
And it's all right, Nurse Halliday, I have no inten-

tion whatsoever of going home.'

'Oh yes you will.' Giles ripped the prescription from the pad. 'And you'll go and get this made out before you leave.'

'I will not!' she snapped, and a stunned Nurse Halliday reflected that this was the first time she'd seen Sister Slater lose her temper—or with a hair out of place. For indeed, a strand of soft dark hair had broken loose from the meticulous French pleat and was wisping across Sister's nose, which in turn was flushed, as was the rest of her normally healthily pale face. 'I'll put my faith in tea and codeine, Nurse. It won't be the first time I've ricked my back.'

'Nor the last, if you don't treat the injury properly,' Giles replied smoothly, and she saw his eyebrow raise a fraction in amusement at the scenario.

'This is too ridiculous for words! Thank you for your time and trouble, Mr Levete, but I'm certainly not going home now, and I shall report for duty as normal tomorrow. And if you won't stop and have a cup of tea with me now, perhaps you ought to think about seeking out Mr Morton and continuing with your exploration of the hospital,' Sister Slater dismissed him with the usual chill in her eyes. Awful man! He was doing it on purpose, she decided as they confronted each other across the office, memories of that tense moment when each had touched a chord in the other forgotten.

'On your head be it, then, Sister. But I'm a doctor, remember, and I recommend that you go home and rest. I always had heard that the nursing profession was notoriously stubborn when it came to themselves being ill. What's the matter, Sister?

Don't you like the idea of relinquishing command
of your little platoon for a couple of days? Worried
that when you get back there'll have been a revolu-
tion on the ward and everyone will be known by
their first names?' And with the ghost of a smile
lurking round his lips, Giles Levete drew himself up
straight, issued a snappy salute, and quick-stepped
from the office.

There, he thought as he made his way up the
corridor, hoping to catch a glimpse of Barney
lurching along, that would put the cat among
the pigeons. Let Sister Slater and her little band
put that in their pipes and smoke it! Still, he
decided more soberly as the euphoria began to die
down, perhaps she wasn't quite the dragon he'd
first suspected. And perhaps he'd been silly to start
so badly with her. If only she wasn't so damned
good at what she did . . .

Still a little gingerly, Louise walked up the garden
path. Cosmo, the tabby that her mother had saved
from a condemned cell at the RSPCA centre, rubbed
round her legs, but today he had no chance of being
stroked. Louise doubted very much if she could
even bend down to him. It was twenty past eight
and the September sun was disappearing fast.
There was even a tang of smoke in the air as the first
bonfires of autumn were lit. Autumn was such a sad
time; it brought back unhappy memories . . .
Never mind, Louise cheered herself, she was home
now, safe in the comfort of the red-brick semi her
mother had bought more than fifteen years ago.
And spring would come again, even if the wait
seemed like an eternity. She let herself in through
the front door and entered the warm hall, Cosmo

following, yowling quietly for his dinner. The house was quiet, peaceful, a haven from the world of the hospital—from the problems of the real world. Sanctuary.

Normally, Louise would have changed upstairs before making herself coffee and having supper. But tonight she didn't feel like climbing stairs until she had to, so she went straight to the pine kitchen, put in only a year or two ago, and flicked on the kettle. With infinite care, she bent at the knees to retrieve Cosmo's empty dish from the floor, rinsed it out and then gave him another serving of Whiskas.

The kitchen was lovely; a big room with lots of windows overlooking the overgrown garden that Louise never seemed to have time to get down to properly. There was a circular pine table and wheelback chairs, and herringbone brick-effect tiles on the floor. In the oven she discovered half a home-made lasagne, almost cold, and she set the oven on to warm it through, suddenly hungry. The kettle boiled and she took two pottery mugs from a cupboard, spooned in instant coffee, added milk and finally water, before going to the bottom of the stairs and calling up to the landing, 'I'm home! Coffee?'

From upstairs came an answering thump as a chair scraped back, and knowing that her message had been received, Louise returned to the kitchen and checked the progress of her supper. There was a clatter of feet as someone raced down the stairs, and then a tall figure with blond hair appeared in the doorway.

'Hello, Mum,' Dan said cheerfully. 'Have a good day at work?'

CHAPTER TWO

SOMETIMES, like now, Louise felt a sort of awe when she watched her son and saw him as others did —tall and straight and full of youthful good looks. How long ago was it since he was a little boy, dependent on her for everything? It seemed hardly yesterday. And yet here he was now, almost seventeen, a young man with ideas and plans of his own. Plans which, she forced herself to accept, would one day not include her. But that was what she wanted for him, wasn't it? University, a fulfilling career . . .

Looking at him now, so tanned and athletic after a holiday with her brother and his family in Crete, Louise felt proud enough to burst. Whatever pain her ill-fated marriage of eighteen years ago had brought, it was all worth it for this—just for the pleasure of having Dan by her side.

'I've had a dreadful day,' she admitted. 'I've strained my back and started off on the wrong foot with a new consultant. But never mind—there's always tomorrow. How about you? Did you get into trouble for leaving your football kit behind? I nearly fell over it in the hall when I went on duty.'

'I know! I had to borrow a pair of shorts from the "lost" cupboard where all the smelly old things no one wants any more get dumped. They were too big and kept falling down, and all the fourth-year girls were out playing netball and kept staring.' Dan Slater had just started in the Upper Sixth at school and was studying for his A levels. What's more, his broad grin told his mother that he didn't mind the interest of the fair sex—and had no problems attracting it, either. His good looks, easy-going temperament and quick mind made him a natural leader at school, where he was in all the sports teams, starred most years in the school play and was well thought of by the teachers. Not that he was too good to be true. In fact Louise often despaired of his late nights practising the electric guitar at a friend's house and the constant stream of companions, increasingly female, who came home with him.

Coming home from a late shift all she wanted, like this evening, was a cup of coffee and some food, *not* half a dozen noisy teenagers trying to make pancakes in the kitchen. But she wasn't so old she'd forgotten what it was like to be seventeen, irresponsible—and in love.

She'd been only a few months older than Dan was now when she'd married Tony Slater, the boy next door, her childhood sweetheart. Her parents had insisted that they wait until Louise had finished her training as a secretary, but once she had her first job, nothing could have held back either her or Tony, who was at art school. Muttering dire warnings, both sets of parents finally gave their consent. Oh, they *had* been in love—so much in love that they were deaf to the warnings and quite blind to the responsibilities that marriage involved. There'd been such hopes, such castles in the air. Louise would support Tony through college, where he was already gaining a promising reputation as a designer. They would have an affluent future together, a beautiful house . . .

And then, suddenly, came the news that Dan was on the way. From the day that Louise had nervously announced her pregnancy, things had started to go wrong. The baby drained her stamina, so she had to forgo all the social activities that were a part of Tony's art school scene in the Swinging Sixties. He began to go out on his own and to gain the confidence he had once lacked and looked to Louise for. And when Dan was born, Tony's genuine delight in his son could not overcome the fact that nappies and feeds and the necessity of his pretty young wife staying at home conflicted with the busy tempo of his career. Tony wanted a dolly-bird, a pretty companion to show off—but try as she might, Louise couldn't look after her son properly *and* go drinking and dancing into the small hours . . .

There had been, at first, a gradual drifting apart; Louise into a world of domesticity, play schools and children, Tony into his world of glamour, fast deals, instant renown. And then had come the rows—rows after he had stayed out all night, rows because Louise couldn't, *wouldn't* leave Dan with a complete stranger while she went off to the opening of some new exhibition or a business dinner party . . .

And then at last had come the confession that her husband had fallen out of love with her, and into love with another woman. A woman who could be all the things he wanted her to be. A woman who wasn't tied down by a baby; didn't have stretch-marks; didn't greet him at the door looking harassed and tired.

Dan was just three years old when the divorce became final. For another three years he had seen his father regularly, for, despite all the problems, the break-up was not as bitter as some; Louise still felt in her heart some of her old affection for her husband, and she didn't want Dan to suffer. So Tony came to the house that Louise's mother had bought in north London each week to see his son, and they tried to get on well, despite the inevitable pain. Then Tony had gone to America and Louise had had Dan to herself, except for flying visits. When he was fourteen Dan flew out to New York to spend a month with his father, and back at home Louise had worried that Tony's money and glamour would seduce their son into leaving her and staying in the States. But no. Dan had thrown himself into her arms at Heathrow and told her how much he'd missed her—and since then, Tony's name was rarely mentioned. Not because he was forgotten, avoided, but because he was irrelevant to their daily lives. He sent birthday cards, Christmas presents, but he didn't phone or write, and their lives were smooth and settled. Dan spent his holidays with Louise's brother's family, which included two boys his own age, so he had plenty of male influence in his life. And until two years ago his grandmother had been around to provide the stable home background that gives a child security and confidence.

When had Louise made the momentous decision never to get involved with another man? Never to jeopardise her son's stable, if unusual, family? When had she become that ice-cool superwoman, Sister Slater? It was difficult to say after all these years. When he was four, Dan had fallen off a swing in the park and sustained a nasty compound fracture that had kept him in hospital for nearly three

weeks. Louise had visited him daily in the ortho-
paedic section of the children's ward and been
fascinated by what she saw. So fascinated that one
afternoon she'd left Dan and gone along and
registered to start her nursing training just as soon
as he started school. With her mother at home and
her sister with her own growing family nearby,
Louise knew it was a mistake to stay at home and
brood on what had happened. She was still young;
there was time to do something really positive with
her life. And so she had coped with the study and
the night shifts and qualified, head of her year, as
an SRN.

Her training taught her more than medical ex-
pertise, though. It taught her how vulnerable she
was, how easily hurt; and how like a leper was a
pretty young woman with a child.

In her third year, still only in her early twenties,
but with a maturity beyond her years that attracted
men like wasps to a jampot, Louise had fallen in
love with a young doctor. He had been the classic
stuff that all young doctors are made of—
handsome, arrogant, pleased with himself for sur-
viving his long apprenticeship—and ready to marry
Staff Nurse Slater with her cool blue eyes and neat
figure and apparent knowledge of what life was all
about. But what he hadn't bargained for was Dan,
seven now, and hostile to any new man in his
mother's life. They had tried to make things work,
but the men in her life seemed unable to get on with
each other, and soon the doctor had departed for
other, less complicated, pastures.

It was then that Louise decided that she would
never again get involved with another man, never
again threaten Dan's security. And so super-

efficient Staff Nurse Slater had arrived at
Highstead Hospital with her testimonials glowing and proceeded to put every other nurse on the
premises to shame. Her reputation spread. Staff
Nurse Slater went home after duty and never went
drinking or dancing with the other young nurses.
Staff Nurse Slater cut every intern, registrar and
consultant dead at the slightest hint of familiarity.
Staff Nurse Slater took her holidays with her civ-
ilian friends and didn't bring back her snaps to show
to everyone. Did anyone see Staff Nurse Slater
crying quietly in the sluice, cut to the quick by
something overheard? Did anyone think to ask the
identity of the young boy whose picture she carried
in her wallet? Did no one ever notice her wistfully
watching young nurses mooning over handsome
housemen and making plans for dates, and wonder
why her eyes sparkled and she turned away? If they
did, they said nothing.

It was not that Dan was a secret. His existence
was known to the authorities, to her seniors—and
after all, a staff nurse with a young son was not so
very unusual as to require remarking upon. If
Louise had occasionally to take a day off to look
after Dan, they tolerated it—her diligence and
competence were beyond complaint. Nor was
Louise actively disliked or resented by anyone at
the hospital. She was too pleasant, too easy to get
on with for that. In fact, there were many admiring
nurses who would have liked to get to know her.
But though she was always polite, she never
seemed to have time for them. If a fellow nurse
invited her to supper at her flat in the nurses' home,
Louise always politely declined—she was, always,
regretfully, busy. If a party was organised to go to

the theatre, Louise was, alas, engaged somewhere else. And so her twenties had passed her by, her youth disappeared, and Dan and her family were compensation enough—most of the time.

Five years ago, *Sister* Slater had emerged. Her natural aloofness at last found its niche. Patients, nurses, doctors—all respected her, trusted her, relied on her, and all knew not to venture their friendship too far for fear of rebuff. All, it seemed, except Giles Levete who, with his mocking comments and laughing eyes and refusal to take anything she said seriously, had been the first to penetrate her armour for years . . .

'Mum! Are you all right? Is your back hurting you? I've got some of that liniment I had for my knee if it'll help.'

Louise struggled back from her daydream of Giles Levete's rich, soothing voice, his hands gently working their way down her back. 'Thanks for the offer, but I don't want to end up smelling like one of the pensioners we get at visiting time in the winter—all eucalyptus and embrocation. I've got some tablets the dispensary made up, don't worry. Check and see if the lasagne's ready, will you?'

'I was too hungry to wait for you,' Dan explained, scooping the shrivelled portion of pasta out of the dish and throwing it on to a cold plate before placing it in front of Louise.

'Cutlery?' she suggested gently before he sat down again, and he brought a knife and two forks —one of which he used himself to steal pieces from her plate.

'Can Martin come and stay at the weekend?' he asked, deliberately casual. Louise knew that tone of voice of old.

'Don't see why not,' she murmured. The lasagne was still only lukewarm in its centre. 'And don't pick my food, Dan! I'm a hard-working woman; I need all the nourishment I can get! Where are you off to at the weekend then?'

Dan got moodily to his feet and went to the bread bin, where he cut himself a doorstep of wholemeal and spread it with peanut butter. Louise wondered how he stayed so enviably svelte—he ate enough to feed a whole rugby team, yet in his faded jeans and black and white lumberjack shirt he was positively rangy. Sexy, even, she thought—should a mother think that of her son? Well, he was. And all the girls who called seemed to think so too. She only hoped he'd treat his physical gifts responsibly. Telling him the facts of life and drumming home the message about love and care being as important as sex was one thing; knowing whether he was actually sowing his wild oats was quite another. She just had to trust him. But knowing how things had been for herself at his age, Louise sympathised.

'We're going to Hammersmith to see Madness,' he revealed at last, picking up Cosmo and cuddling him like a baby. No, not a baby; Dan wouldn't deign to pick up a baby!

'I don't want to seem like a nagging mother—'

'But you don't want me to go! *Why?*' He turned on her almost violently. 'Hammersmith isn't the ends of the earth, you know—and I'm quite capable of looking after myself. I'm seventeen, you know!'

'You're sixteen,' Louise retaliated, 'and if you're trekking off to the other side of London late at night of course I worry. Would you really like it if

I didn't? What happens if you miss the last tube home?'

'We get a taxi back—or a late-night bus. Credit me with some sense, Mum! I know when you were sixteen you had to be home and in bed by ten, but things are different now. None of the things I want to do finish before ten . . . And I'm not going to get run over by a bus or inveigled away by some creep!'

There were other fears Louise had, of course. Fears that would have inflamed Dan's adolescent contempt even further. But he'd never been on duty on a Saturday night in a London Casualty department. He'd not seen less fortunate young men who'd got drunk and then into fights; glue sniffers, drug addicts . . . Calm down, Louise reminded herself. Drug addicts and glue sniffers weren't boys like Dan, from a good home, with friends and prospects. And anyway, they formed a tiny part of a casualty department's intake. Even so, her exposure to the hard facts of the real world had made her more aware of what a sixteen-year-old on a Saturday night could get up to than most mothers. And it made being a mother that much more difficult.

'All right. You know I trust you.' She tried to play the argument down. 'Make sure you've got enough money, and if you get stuck, call me and I'll come and pick you up.'

'Yes ma'am!' He stood to attention, raised his sandwich to his ear in a crisp salute, and clicked his heels—and Louise felt an involuntary cringe rise inside her. First Giles Levete and now her own son. Was she such a harridan that *everyone* felt they had to kow-tow to her? If only they understood that she *had* to be like this because she cared . . . That she didn't want to be the cold, bossy creature that they all saw, but that someone had to give the orders, put a foot down. And it was always her. Sister and single parent. Tough roles to fulfil.

With a change of subject to distract her, Dan announced, 'The new people have moved in next door. I saw them when I came back from school. The chap looked all right—said hallo to me. They've got a chaise longue just like ours, so they must be OK.'

'I expect we'll introduce ourselves in time,' Louise said. 'They've got to be easier to live with than the Maddoxes, anyway.'

The Maddoxes had been a difficult elderly couple, forever in need of assistance in the form of lifts to the shops, spare light bulbs or someone young and agile enough to climb into the loft and inspect their water tank. Louise and Dan had complied as far as they could, but that did not prevent the Maddoxes complaining if Dan so much as turned on his stereo after eight in the evening or had a few friends round in the garden. Even Louise had lost her temper with them a few months ago when they'd come round one Saturday evening to complain that Dan was making a racket—for he had been out at a friend's! Adolescent boys seemed to attract trouble of that sort, though, and Louise had learnt to discount tales of Dan's mischief.

'Perhaps we ought to invite them in for a drink?' she wondered aloud. 'Although if they're as smart as you seem to think they are . . .'

Her gaze took in the well-used furniture. Apart from the chaise longue, which Louise had re-upholstered not so long ago and had been stunned to discover that it was worth nearly seven hundred pounds, they didn't have anything worth crowing about. Sometimes she wondered about the hideous Chinese vase, left by the same aunt who had bequeathed Louise the chaise longue, but it was so horrible, an eyesore on the hall table, that she doubted it.

'Have you finished your homework?' she asked as she pushed away the last remains of the lasagne.

'Yes.' Dan's tone had a world-weary 'Don't I always do my homework' edge to it, and he got up from the table as the telephone rang. 'That's bound to be Tracy Armitage, desperate to whisper sweet nothings in my ear,' he leched as he went to answer it.

'Ah, Sister, thank goodness you're back.' Staff Nurse Simpson hurried out of the nurses' station to greet Louise, who had spent a tedious hour at a Sisters' meeting.

'Problems, Rosie?' Louise dumped the clipboard and the sheaf of notes about the ordering of dangerous drugs, and turned to the worried face of her plump staff nurse.

'Mrs Bradbury wants to discharge herself. She's been almost hysterical for the last forty minutes. Apparently her mother phoned and told her some old wives' tale, and now she wants to go home.'

'She's due in theatre tomorrow,' Louise ran down the relevant lists. 'I'll talk to her. Perhaps you could get on to her doctor and see if he'll prescribe a tranquilliser. Anything else?'

'Yes. Women's Medical have called twice. They've got an urgent peptic ulcer they want brought over immediately. I told them we don't have a bed . . .'

'Damn. Miss Callaghan? She could go.' Louise flicked through the Kardex on her desk which gave details of all the patients currently on the ward. 'No, she can't. Mr Amery talked to me yesterday about the necessity of getting the social worker to see her before she goes out.'

'Of course, if we allowed Mrs Bradbury to go . . .' Nurse Simpson suggested.

'No, we've got her and we'll keep her until that investigation has been done and we know what the shadow on her X-ray is,' Louise squashed the suggestion firmly. 'Arkwright—that's the one. Call Mr Amery, we'll need her papers signed pronto. And while you're at it, Rosie, see if Medical will do a swop—peptic ulcer for Mrs Elsdon.'

'Lovely! Poor Mrs Elsdon—it's not really her fault that no one wants her!'

Twenty minutes later, one matter, at least, had been settled. Mrs Arkwright, who had bounced back after her cholecystectomy, was sent packing a couple of days earlier than she might have been, and her jubilant husband was on his way to collect her by the time Mr Amery signed the discharge slip. SEN Bryant, a cheerful West Indian girl, helped her to pack up her things and then set about preparing the bed for its next occupant. Through the pink floral curtains that had been drawn around Mrs Bradbury's bed, Nurse Bryant could hear Sister Slater's firm tones as she persuaded her patient that running away from the hospital would do no one any good. Mrs Bradbury was first indignant, then downright abusive—and finally she broke down into sobs on Sister's steady shoulder. Tucking in her corners expertly, and making sure all the openings of her pillow slips faced away from the ward doors, Nurse Bryant smiled to herself. It was no good arguing with Sister Slater—she could have told Mrs Bradbury that at any time! She might have been able to put Rosie Simpson, who was too soft-hearted for her own good, in a dither, but Sister Slater? Never!

'Mrs Bradbury will be staying with us.' Louise emerged brushing at the damp patch on her blue uniform. 'I'm sure she'd appreciate a cup of tea, Nurse Bryant. And I expect there's something to calm her down in the office. And, Nurse, I hope that you're going to sterilise that water jug and refill it before our next patient arrives?'

'Yes, Sister, straight away.' Nurse Bryant's smile faded a little. It was difficult to feel warmly towards Sister for long. Thank goodness, though, she hadn't taken a look inside the locker and seen all the old tissues and sweet wrappers still to be cleaned out!

Louise walked swiftly around her ward, arranging a bed-table here, a vase of flowers there, checking that Mrs Higgins's drip was flowing properly and that Mrs Elsdon was upright enough, and generally ensuring that everyone was content. Mrs Narasimhan's fluid intake was low, and Louise cajoled her into taking a tumbler of lemon barley water while she chatted and checked the patient's other vital signs. Caroline Hilton, a young woman who had made it clear from her first day on the ward that she was only here under sufferance because her private insurance scheme had let her down, requested a proper bath—and had to accept

Louise's calm assurance that she was not yet ready for one.

'You *have* had a sponge bath this morning?' Louise asked flatly.

'Yes, but I want to wallow in a tub for half an hour,' Miss Hilton insisted petulantly. 'I'm used to bathing properly every day.'

'I'm sure we all are.' Louise's voice was just astringent enough to check the younger woman. 'But the fact is that after half an hour in a bath your stitches would probably have floated away. And it certainly wouldn't do that neat little scar of yours any good at all. So please accept my advice, Miss Hilton, and persevere with the sponge baths.'

With pouting silence her only response, Sister Slater moved on to Miss Callaghan, one of her favourite patients. Miss Callaghan had come to Highstead nearly four months ago now, first to have a hip joint replaced and then to have a kidney problem treated surgically. It would only be a few days now before she went home—and Louise knew that she would sorely miss the life and stimulation of the ward. A retired school teacher, Miss Callaghan had hardly a penny to her name and was living in a council development in St Pancras. It was not the sort of environment Louise would have had any of her patients suffer, and particularly not Miss Callaghan, who was sitting disconsolately in bed.

'Good morning, Miss Callaghan. I haven't seen you walking the wards today. Is your hip troubling you?' Louise asked with surprising gentleness.

'Oh no, Sister!' The woman's shrewd, watery blue eyes expressed both her delight at being able to walk again—and her apprehension. 'I was just thinking that it won't be long before I have to say goodbye to all of you. I wonder, Sister, if you can help me. I'd like to have my hair set before I go home, and I know that there's someone who comes round to do it . . .'

'Yes?' Louise prompted, 'I can certainly make an appointment for you.'

'Do you know if it's terribly expensive, Sister? It's just that I find it so difficult to do myself, and it would be so nice not to have to worry about it.'

Louise's smile took in the cheap cotton night-dress with its lace fraying from wear, the absence of flowers or fruit on the bedside locker and the carefully ironed handkerchief laid out for use— more economical than wasteful tissues, and laundered each week by Miss Callaghan's equally elderly sister who lived not far from the hospital.

'Oh, the hairdressing service is quite free,' she lied. 'I'll make an appointment for tomorrow, shall I?'

With her patient's thanks still in her ears, she continued down the neat ward to her office and telephoned the hairdresser herself. 'Come and see me, will you, Deirdre, before you go to Miss Callaghan?' It was a request that the hairdresser had heard once or twice before from Sister Slater and understood well. Before going back to her staff nurses and informing them of Mrs Bradbury's change of heart, Louise opened her desk draw, sorted through the small collection of items she had been given as thank-you presents, and extracted a box of soap and one of assorted chocolates. She hailed the SEN who was passing her door.

'Nurse Bryant, would you take these to Miss

Callaghan and tell her that Mrs Arkwright left them behind and we don't want them wasted?'

With a grin, Naomi Bryant set off down the ward. Oh, Starchy Slater wasn't *all* bad! If only she'd prove herself human and enjoy it a bit more . . .

Louise sat down at her desk and began to sort through the paperwork piled in a heap, waiting for her attention. This was the only thing she regretted about being made up to a Sister—the paperwork. Sometimes there were whole days when she hardly saw her patients, and with her band of responsible staff nurses available, there wasn't much necessity for Louise's nursing skills. Highstead didn't have a training school and so all the nurses on the wards, apart from the odd few who were seconded by their city hospitals a few miles up the road, were qualified. That meant that Louise didn't have the teaching responsibilities or nursing demands that other Sisters might have. Her staff, like Rosie Simpson, were experienced and responsible and quite capable of doing all they were required to do without supervision. Sometimes Louise regretted it, but then she couldn't have coped with anything more demanding with Dan on her hands. Perhaps when he went to university she'd try for a position where she could nurse more regularly . . .

Meanwhile, there was the fortnightly laundry slip to countersign—a matter of great urgency and importance! Louise ran her pen down the columns of figures. That couldn't be right! She checked again, then took the calculator from a drawer and added it all up mechanically. How had they used 161 sheets and only 27 pillowslips? Nurse Rees must have made an error somewhere. Well, there was one immediate check to be carried out.

With the chit in her hands, Louise made her way to the linen room. And she didn't have to pull anything from the shelves to know at a glance that Nurse Rees's calculation was quite wrong. If they'd used all those sheets there would be nothing left on the shelf, yet—

'Hello, Louise. Escaping from the pressures of running your platoon?'

Giles Levete's sarcastic tones interrupted her thoughts and she swung round to find him lounging just outside the door, still with that indefinably scruffy look about him, still with that infuriating twinkle in his eye.

Louise's hackles rose. No one called her by her Christian name—not even Professor Barnet! 'As you can see perfectly well, I'm just checking the linen,' she managed coldly. 'And I do not run a platoon here, Mr Levete. I run a ward. Is there anything I can assist you with? Have you come to see a patient, perhaps?'

'No. I came to talk over the post-operative care of some of my patients—and to enquire if your back is better.'

'I'm fine, thank you,' she snapped, remembering all too well what had happened last week and mistrusting the half smile that lurked around his mouth.

'I can make another examination,' he suggested, entering the linen room, which was cramped at the best of times, and leaned casually against a pile of blankets—which promptly gave way and threw him off his balance. Grabbing one of the shelves for support, he managed to right himself for a moment before that, too, collapsed under the strain and deposited him on the floor amid a small mountain of mattress covers.

'Oh dear, Mr Levete! What an unfortunate accident . . .' Louise bent to retrieve the covers and to help him to his feet, laughter and relief bubbling beneath her words. 'Are you all right—or would you like to go straight to my office so that my nurses and I can check you over?' she murmured slyly. At least the man had the grace to look bashful, she decided, as he climbed to his feet.

'Damn. Anything remotely domestic and I'm a walking disaster area,' he said, as much to himself as to Louise. 'My daughter always says—'

Louise had been hastily gathering the mattress covers into a semblance of tidiness, but she stopped dead at his final words, uttered so unexpectedly. He had a daughter; therefore he had a wife. She felt a tight knot of irrational disappointment lodge in the pit of her stomach, irrational because she had thought of Giles Levete for the past day or two with nothing more than a vague sense of annoyance that he could disturb her equilibrium. She had certainly not lain awake at night conjecturing about his marital or domestic status. So why was it such a shock?

'Don't worry,' she muttered, suddenly resuming her activity.

'I can't imagine you letting off one of your nurses so lightly, Louise,' Giles ventured sharply. He felt a fool, even though he'd been able to get to his feet rather elegantly. Why had he mentioned his daughter? Louise Slater had registered the fact, he knew, and that infuriated him. He didn't quite know where he wanted to go or how he wanted his relationship with this enigmatic, cold-eyed woman to develop. But the mention of a child always frightened women off—particularly a daughter, whom they imagined to be competition. Giles checked himself again; it sounded as if he'd got designs on this cool, sanctimonious woman tidying round his feet as if her life depended on it. God, if that wasn't the last thing he wanted!

'Feel free to tick me off in any way you think appropriate, Sister,' he retaliated, and there was something like real hostility in his blue eyes when she looked up. 'Forty lashes? A court martial? Keel-hauling, perhaps, though that might pose difficulties. . . .'

'Don't be so stupid!' It had been said before Louise had even thought. It was what she'd have said to Dan if he'd behaved so badly, or to one of her nurses. So why not to this consultant who should, after all, know better? And whoever his wife was, Louise thought darkly as she stood up, she ought to look after him better than she did, because the hem of his trousers was beginning to fray where it was rubbing on the top of his expensive but not recently polished shoe.

'I don't know what you've been told about me, Mr Levete, but if you care to look around my ward you will see that it is happy, efficient and successful. There are no nurses strung from the rafters for their transgressions, no patients in manacles because they failed to ask for a bedpan in time, and no one in solitary confinement because they have failed to please me. And as a consultant surgeon you should be very pleased,' she took a breath, 'because it means your patients will have the best attention you could possibly expect. I don't play games, Mr Levete—I'm just a good sister.'

'Have I suggested that you aren't?' he responded quietly. 'Louise, I—'

'*Sister Slater*, Mr Levete, if you please. And if you would still care to discuss your patients and the special nursing they require, you are welcome to do so—in my room.' With a dignity that she fought hard to maintain, Louise stepped past him and into the corridor. Let him follow her to her office if he would. The sound of leather soled shoes clattering in the shining corridor seemed to accompany her for a moment, and then faded. Giles Levete had headed in the other direction and left the ward.

CHAPTER THREE

'MY GOD! What on earth have you had for your supper?' Louise surveyed the take-away wrappers and empty packets on the kitchen table aghast.

'Burger and chips and a milkshake, and then we bought treacle tart and ice-cream from the shop on the corner,' Dan confessed. 'And Coke, and a Mars bar each . . .'

'Well, when you both get covered in acne and have heart attacks at the age of forty, don't blame me.'

'Actually, Mrs Slater,' Martin, Dan's friend who had been quietly sitting back from the conversation, chimed in, 'it's been proved that acne isn't affected by diet, it's hereditary. And there is a growing lobby who believe that all this fuss over cholesterol has been blown up out of all proportion.'

'Well,' Louise digested all this and conceded that as Martin was studying to go to medical school he probably *did* have a grain of truth in his theories, 'try telling that to all the coronary cases I see at work.' That silenced them. In fact she'd had a good day for silencing people all round. First Giles Levete, who'd loped off the ward and hadn't been seen again, and now these gannets.

'We're going out now,' Dan announced. 'I've made up a bed for Martin in the back room.'

'Where are you off to?' Louise asked almost

automatically as she filled the kettle and scooped
Whiskas for Cosmo.

'*Mum!*' Dan's pained look said a lot. Martin
raised a sympathetic eyebrow. Parents were a real
pain. Dan was lucky only to have the one to cope
with.

'What if Tracy Armitage calls and wants to
know where you are?' Louise asked innocently. 'If
I don't know where you are, how can I tell her
where to meet you?'

'If *she* calls don't you dare tell her where I am,'
Dan hastily corrected her. 'I'm not going out with
her any more, but I want to let her down nicely. I'm
going round to Rebecca's this evening, but don't
tell her that. Just say you don't know.'

'And who's Rebecca?' Louise began to scrunch
up the burger papers, dripping with grease, and
drop them in the bin.

'She's a new girl at school,' Martin explained
diplomatically. 'Her parents aren't around much
and we're allowed to go round to her house and
have a bit of a party in the evenings.' He named an
address not five minutes' walk away.

'OK, just so long as I know where you are,'
Louise said without further fuss. 'I don't have to tell
you to behave yourselves, do I?'

'No, we're good boys,' Dan confirmed without
much conviction. 'Go and get your jacket, Martin,
and we'll be off.' They didn't look much like good
boys, Louise thought privately. Martin hulked
around in a black leather jacket and a glorified
string vest to show off his fuzzy chest and Dan's
oversized jacket, slicked-back hair and purposely
baggy black trousers made him look like a Forties
lounge lizard. Still, they were both clean and

relatively tidy, and at least they took an interest
in their appearance. And she'd once worn a mini
skirt that had been little more than a belt herself,
remember!

She quite expected the knock at the door to be
another crony done up to the nines for this Friday
night party, but in fact a neat-looking sandy-haired
man with a small moustache was waiting on the
doorstep.

'Hello,' he smiled very broadly, offering his hand
before introducing himself in a gesture that Louise
thought a bit dubious. Double-glazing, encyclo-
paedias and loft extensions she certainly didn't
need.

'I'm afraid I . . .'

'Victor Inskip, your new neighbour. Pleased to
meet you,' he pumped away on her wrist heartily.
And before Louise quite knew how he'd done it, he
was standing in the hall and looking round him with
an observant eye.

'Louise Slater,' Louise heard herself saying as
she wondered wildly whether it would be appropriate to invite him in for drinks. 'Oh, and my son
Dan, and Martin.'

Victor Inskip did a slight double-take at the
vision of adolescent cool that met his eyes, but
pumped them firmly by the hand too, and called
them 'boys' in a patronising fashion that had them
both looking down their noses at him.

'I just popped round to let you know that you're
all invited for a few drinks tomorrow evening, a sort
of house-warming party,' he informed them in a
voice that was a little too gushing for comfort.

'Thank you,' Louise said, trying to sound as
grateful as the invitation had implied she should be.

Dan and Martin lurked silently on the stairs looking sulky. 'I expect "the boys",' Louise said slightly ironically, 'are already busy, I'm afraid.'

'We're going to Hammersmith,' Martin reminded her in a voice an octave lower than it had been when he'd last spoken to her.

'Really?' Mr Inskip had manoeuvred himself across the hall and was peering into the sitting-room. 'I see you've got that nice little bay window still there,' he observed. 'The Maddoxes were great ones for improvement, I'm afraid, and took theirs out. Very nice chaise longue you've got there, Mrs Slater.'

'Thank you,' Louise replied coolly, certain now that this man was not going to get the chance to stay any longer than politeness required. 'Who knows, if I have a spare moment, I may pop round to share a welcoming glass of wine with you.' Oh no I will not, she decided firmly.

Victor Inskip was not an unpleasant man to look at. He had a good physique, in fact was surprisingly tall, and his sandy hair and moustache were neatly kept—not like one blond-haired consultant Louise could name! But his eyes were somehow piercingly shrewd, and when he smiled he was all teeth but no warmth in the rest of his face. There was something calculating about him, something thick-skinned, which seemed to say, 'I know I'm not wanted here but I'm not going before *I'm* ready to go.' Louise had met men like this before in the Casualty department at the hospital; men who were so ordinary-looking that they were almost extraordinary, but who were often violent or unpredictable in their behaviour. After all, one look at a man like Giles Levete, all those angles to his lean face and that riotous hair, and one expected something a bit anarchic. But not from someone like Victor Inskip. Nevertheless, it was the latter who made Louise's hackles rise highest.

'Well,' he'd obviously seen enough, 'it's nice to meet you. I'm relying on seeing you there, Louise.' He made her name sound insinuating. 'And Mr Slater, too, of course.'

'I'm afraid my husband's in the States at the moment,' Louise said with the merest margin of truth, hoping that Dan wouldn't contradict her. But somehow she didn't want this man to know she was divorced; he was just the sort who'd decide that his services were needed.

'Never mind, you're very welcome on your own. Goodbye to you all.' And then he'd gone, almost as rapidly as he'd arrived.

'There was no need for you to hang around, "boys",' she laughed, and there was a slight touch of nervousness in her voice.

'We weren't going to walk off and leave you with *that* creep in the house, were we?' Dan said defensively, coming down the stairs. 'You be all right on your own here, Mum?' Despite the fact that Martin was present and his macho dignity compromised, he put an arm round her shoulder.

'Of course I will,' Louise slapped his bottom playfully. 'Go on—go off to Rebecca's and enjoy yourselves, but remember—don't do anything there you wouldn't do here. And home by midnight. You've both got your Saturday jobs to go to in the morning.'

'Yes, Mum. No, Mum.' Dan gave her a peck on the cheek and they slouched out, ready to terrify old ladies on the street.

*   *   *

'If we went to Administration *en masse*, with our requests organised, they'd have to take some notice of us, surely?' Sister Walsh stood in front of the mirror in the Sisters' changing room and adjusted the angle of her cap, a white hair grip waggling at the corner of her mouth as she spoke awkwardly to Louise, who was crouched down lacing up her shoes.

'I suppose so,' she agreed, 'but what with cut-backs and everything, do we really have any chance of getting ward clerks? If it's a choice between nurses and administrators, let's have nurses every time. I know it's tiresome, having to do all the paperwork, but when the crunch comes, you and I can turn our hands to caring for the patients, too. I wouldn't let a ward clerk give an injection!'

'I still think it's got out of hand—particularly on the surgical wards, where the paperwork is so much more complicated,' Sister Walsh continued. She was the head of Men's Surgical, a rather hard-faced woman with a reputation for encouraging the wandering eyes of any of the doctors. A good enough nurse and quite justified in her complaint about the amount of administration expected of sisters, but Louise didn't really want to get involved. Walsh could sometimes take forcefulness too far, to the edge of rudeness, and she tended to have favourites and non-favourites among her staff. To be on the wrong side of Sister Walsh was to be very unhappy, so some of Louise's staff would have it.

It was a quarter past seven, and already sounds of activity were beginning to buzz on the air as night staff finished the job of washing and breakfasting those newly awakened patients unfortunate enough to have been kept in hospital over the weekend. Louise didn't mind early shifts, except when she was very tired. Getting up before six and coming in to work on the bus wasn't much fun if you hadn't had much sleep the night before. But you got used to it. She rather liked the deserted feel of the building at this time of the morning before out patients and visitors and the hundred and one nine-to-fivers arrived.

From the window of the changing room—all staff at Highstead were expected to change on site to avoid the dangers of contamination on public transport—she could see the squared-off shape of the new Seymour Unit, specially designed to receive burns and reconstructive surgery cases. It was nearly finished and would be opening in a week or two. Perhaps, she wondered, she had been a fool not to apply for a Sister's post there? But with fewer patients it would probably not be as interesting as the constantly changing pattern of life on Women's Surgical.

'Why don't you suggest the idea to Admin,' Louise murmured, straightening her own cap, 'and then we'll see. But I *would* like someone to do the basics like the laundry dockets and standard drug orders for me. Having to make out forms every time we need new soap is beginning to get me down!'

'Speaking of laundry,' Sister Walsh interrupted, 'how are you getting along with the new cardiologist, Mr Levete?'

'What he's got to do with laundry I can't imagine,' Louise replied, flustered. 'I find him a little too flippant for my taste.'

'Quite a wit, isn't he?' Walsh looked at her

narrowly in the mirror but said nothing about the incident in the linen room that someone must have spotted. 'But I *had* heard that you and he didn't quite hit it off. Never mind, I'm sure he gets a warm enough welcome elsewhere in the hospital.'

'I'm sure he does,' Louise agreed through gritted teeth, before turning neatly on her heel and walking out.

'There's a policeman outside the ward doors! What on earth's going on?'

The night staff nurse finished putting the final touches to the records and filing the shift's paper-work before answering Louise.

'We had a late night admission to the ward. Police brought her in after she was left at the station. They reckon there's something to do with a taking and driving offence and they want to interview her. I told them they weren't coming in until breakfasts were over and the kid was properly awake,' she said with a tough glint in her eye. 'Here at all hours of the day and night just wanting to have a word with her! They'd have been quite happy to interview her as soon as she came round from the anaesthetic.'

'Who's her surgeon? And what's wrong with her?' Louise dumped her bag and began flicking through the Kardex.

'Higgins, Lucy, aged sixteen. Nothing major. Broken ribs and punctured lung and a dislocation of the right shoulder. She'll live. Mr Levete was called in to do it and was very tetchy about the whole thing.'

'I don't suppose he reckoned on having to come out to an emergency in his first week. It's not

as if we've got a proper Casualty department, is
it?'

'He's nice, really—makes you want to look after
him, Sister. And he's very relaxed about things.
But he certainly has a temper,' the staff nurse
rambled.

'He's a mite too relaxed about everything, in my
opinion,' Louise murmured under her breath. 'Are
you ready to give report?' She opened the door.
Yes, Jenny, Carolyn and Rosie and the two auxiliaries were there, her regulars, and another SEN as
well. A good job, too. It looked as if it was going to
be a busy day.

The change-over completed, Louise went to
check on her patients and spent a few minutes with
the lively Lucy Higgins, who was quite well awake
now. Even so, she'd have to be checked by Mr
Levete or whoever was on duty before the policeman was allowed in to talk to her, Louise decided.
Because she hadn't been well enough to see her
parents for very long the night before, Louise also
offered to allow them in to see Lucy this morning.
There was nothing major on, and it would serve to
put their minds at rest. How worried they must be
to think of their young daughter lying here in bed,
victim, so it seemed, of some sort of hit and run. A
shudder of sympathy for them ran through Louise;
she hoped that Dan had got up in time to get to
work.

Checking her watch, she excused herself and
went back to the office to ring him, just to make
sure. He answered irritably—yes, he was up and on
his way out right now . . . That done, Louise went
to the ward doors and told the young constable
there that he might as well go back to the police

station for a while, because he wouldn't see Lucy until she'd been checked and confirmed fit enough for interview by a doctor. He was argumentative and took some persuading, but eventually agreed to return after lunch.

'She's not going to walk out of here, I promise you,' Louise told him, smiling.

'Just you make sure she doesn't try,' he'd said humourlessly.

By the time she returned to the ward, the morning's routine was going nicely. Jenny Rees was already mopping up a pool of water she had spilled while doing a dressings change on an ulcer, so everything was running true to form. Louise glowered half-heartedly as she went by, but the girl was so embarrassed that it was difficult to feel more than just rueful about it.

Mrs Dixon's drip was a bit sluggish and Louise quickly resited it, so the flow was uninterrupted, while Rosie deftly changed the gauze over the gallstones wound. Rosie might look like a tank on manoeuvres as she trundled her trolley down the ward, making the flower vases tremble and the bedcovers flap gently in her wake, but she was an excellent nurse, patient, calm and motherly, quite unintimidating, one who made the patients relaxed and confident. Perhaps the fact that she wasn't a glamorous young thing was part of her secret. Too often the older women on the ward, tired, run down by their illness or unable to tend themselves as they wished after an operation, resented the pert, pretty young nurses who cared for them.

Across the ward Louise heard someone retching and coughing, and stepped out of the cubicle to see who was having trouble. Nurse Halliday was already on her way to Miss Osborne's bed but saw Sister, gave a brief nod and went back to the patient she was bed-bathing.

Louise casually made her way across the ward, stopping for a moment to check Mrs Narasimhan's fluid output chart which looked very unpredictable indeed, and bypassing Miss Hilton, who was lying flat out with her personal stereo headphones on. An annoying, tinny buzz surrounded her, and it probably wasn't a coincidence that the patients in the beds around her had taken themselves off to the day room to watch Swap Shop on the television. Louise wondered whether she dare mention the fact that the headphones weren't adequate to the volume the music was being played but decided to leave well alone. Miss Hilton was a real problem and she didn't want more trouble than was strictly necessary.

Miss Osborne, who had been brought down to the ward from Medical prior to operation on her peptic ulcer, tried vainly to pretend that nothing had happened and to hide the tissue she had coughed into.

'You don't sound too happy to me, Miss Osborne,' Louise smiled. 'Are you all right, my dear? Has the gastrotomy left you with a sore throat?'

'It has, actually,' the lady confided. 'And you ought to know, Sister, that I've started to cough up a few specks of blood.' She sighed, handing over the tissue. Louise checked. Yes, just a few specks. But she might be swallowing more than she was coughing up, so a doctor ought to be alerted and a careful check kept on her stools, just in case. Useful though the gastroscope might be in cases such as this, it could sometimes do more harm than good and bring on a haemorrhage that wouldn't otherwise happen.

'I don't think there are any problems,' she assured the patient. 'I'll get you one of those lozenges you had yesterday to anaesthetise your throat before the tube was put down, if you like. They certainly work very well—but you won't be able to have anything to eat or drink for several hours afterwards, like yesterday, in case you burn yourself or can't swallow. Is your throat bad enough to put up with that?'

'Oh, no—it was a very strange feeling yesterday,' Miss Osborne laughed. 'And I'm not going without my lunch today!'

'Perhaps we can find something a bit less drastic, then. Would a nice cup of tea do you any good?'

'Ooh, yes! I can drink any amount of tea.'

'I'll go and arrange some then. Would you like a cup of tea, Mrs Narasimhan?' Louise called as she filled in the chart at the end of Miss Osborne's bed. The Indian lady shook her head shyly and looked away, and Louise went once more to look at the record of her fluid output. According to the chart she'd drunk more than a litre in the last twelve hours, yet she'd not passed anything at all. Her temperature was normal and she seemed alert enough . . .

'She's bin nippin' out to the toilet at night, while those other nurses bin busy,' Mrs Hooper said clearly, showing all her gums as she spoke—for unlike the more reticent patients who fought to keep their teeth even in the operating theatre, Mrs Hooper only wore her teeth at mealtimes. Otherwise they lived in a pink plastic pot by her bed and frightened young doctors who she urged to take a sweet from her 'jar'.

'Oh dear, is this true?' Mrs Narasimhan looked so sheepish that there was no doubt about the truth of Mrs Hooper's claim. Louise tried patiently to explain why her urine output needed such close monitoring. Mrs Narasimhan had had a partial nephrectomy after she'd sustained injuries to her spleen and kidneys. She'd spent some time on a dialysis machine up in ICU, but now she seemed to be recovering. Still, the renal specialist was worried that a further operation might be necessary, and a good urine output that could be tested in a laboratory to see how things were going was vital to his knowledge. All this Louise tried to make clear, sitting gently on the side of the bed with her patient. But Mrs Narasimhan's English wasn't very good and she wondered just how much was getting through. A Gujerati-speaking nurse would have to be found somewhere to explain, and if the worst came to the worst they'd have to put sides on the bed so that the patient couldn't get out . . . It wasn't fair to blame the nurses for not spotting her. They'd had enough on their hands last night, by the sound of it.

'Morning, Sister. You scared off the long arm of the law, I see. No squad cars waiting to whisk my patient off to jail?' Giles Levete, looking as usual as if he'd just had a satisfactory night out on the tiles, stood towering above her, the slight cleft in his chin made more noticeable by the fact that he'd nicked himself while shaving and had a tiny spot of dried blood sitting in its hollow. That was likely to give his patients lots of confidence, Louise decided.

'I simply told them that there was no point in

hanging around,' she bridled, issuing instructions
to Naomi to make a cup of tea for Miss Osborne.
'Not too hot, please,' she added. And for Giles's
benefit, 'Possible oesophagal haemorrhage—she
had a gastrotomy yesterday.'

'Do you want me to take a look?' he asked in
a rich, lazy voice.

'If you've got a moment on the way out,' she
accepted the offer lightly, as if it was neither here
nor there to her, even though she'd feel relieved.
'You've come to see Miss Higgins, I presume?'

'That's right. If *you* don't have an objection,
Sister?' And all of a sudden that vague edge of real
dislike was in his voice again, and Louise was left
wondering what she'd said wrong now. Except that
it wasn't now he was annoyed about, was it? she
suddenly remembered as she self-consciously
preceded him down the ward. How on earth
could she have forgotten the debacle of their last
meeting? The memory made her blush and she
pretended to be inspecting her fob watch as she
walked.

Behind her Giles Levete fumed. How could she
call a poor young thing like Lucy Higgins *Miss* in
such a manner? Surely the girl would feel even less
comfortable than she was already, bearing in mind
her physical condition, if such starchy rule of law
surrounded her. And look at Louise Slater now
—peering at her watch, wondering just how long
she could allow him to disrupt her confounded
routine!

'For goodness' sake, Sister!' He caught up with
her in a single rangy stride. 'I won't be a split second
longer than I have to. Don't think it suits me to
have to come in on a Saturday morning.' The words

were growled out into her ear, to fox eavesdrop-
pers, and she turned, a genuine look of confusion
on her face.

'I've no intention of hurrying you, Mr Levete.'
Of course, he wouldn't want to hang around, she
realised with a slight pang. He had a wife and
daughter, didn't he? Perhaps they wanted to go
shopping or out somewhere for the day. It hurt
even more to know that she didn't have that sort of
family life now Dan was older. She saw little of him
at the weekends and they didn't go shopping
together any more . . . They didn't do an awful lot
together any more, really.

Lucy Higgins managed a wan smile from her bed.
She was an absolute charmer, despite her bruised
blue eyes and the fact that she was connected to an
underwater sealed bottle that languished beneath
the bed. She had very black hair cut in a gamine
urchin fashion, and a mischievous twinkle about
her.

'Hello, Lucy,' Louise went to the bed and automatically pulled the cover straight, a fact that did
not escape Giles Levete's censorious eye. 'This is
the doctor who saw you last night. Do you remember him?'

'I don't, I'm afraid,' the patient managed.
'Hello.' She nodded to Giles. 'Sister, you know you
said my parents could come in this morning if they
wanted to?' Louise nodded, tidying the bedside
locker and repositioning items so that Lucy could
reach them with her uninjured arm. Giles stood
frowning at them both, redundant. 'Well, as it was
kind of you to offer, and I know we're not normally
allowed visitors until the afternoon, I won't put you
out. A few hours won't make much difference. It

was lovely of you to want to help, though . . .'

Lovely? Kind? Putting Sister out? It was with difficulty Mr Levete held his tongue. Damn it, he'd been the one to save this girl's life, and here she was, soft-soaping Sister and hoping she hadn't put *her* out! And yet almost at once he felt a shaft of reassurance that Sister wasn't the ogre he'd got her down as, and simultaneously a nasty thought. Why, if he was as indifferent to her as he should be, was he so willing to think the worst of her? Well, from now on, he wouldn't let her rile him in any way. He would make sure he was definitely indifferent.

'Hmmm.' He cleared his throat and the two women looked up, as if they'd forgotten for a moment that he was there. 'I'd just like to check the drain, and if things are going well we'll have it out.'

Louise quickly drew the curtains and went off to fetch the trolley so that the dressing could be changed. She was back within a minute, to find Giles Levete sitting on the bed, apparently swopping jokes with his patient and roaring away companionably. Well, she supposed that if he had a daughter he'd know what to talk about. After all, couldn't she hold a conversation about the merits of *The Face* against the *NME*? A fashion-conscious son was one way of keeping on one's toes, she supposed.

'I have everything ready.' Giles dragged himself away from his amusing young patient and joined her to scrub his hands. Louise pulled back the cover and gently lifted the hospital gown, expecting Lucy to become reticent now she was half naked in front of them. But she was as chatty as she could be, given the circumstances, and for the first time

Louise felt a slight misgiving that perhaps their charming, innocent young patient was not quite as naive as she seemed.

Giles examined the ribs, which were bruised, but seemed satisfied with them, and after examining the contents of the bottle and listening to the girl's lungs, he expressed his intention of removing the tube.

Louise helped him into a white coat and drew up the mild local injection they would use to avoid discomfort, before swabbing the spot with an antiseptic solution. Then Giles, hands gloved, quickly removed the tube that had been used to drain and reinflate the lung, and used a single suture to close the puncture wound. It was over quickly and cleanly, for the two medics worked together as if they were a long-established team. Louise was aware of having the instruments at hand a second before Giles reached for them; of knowing with some innate sense what he would want next and where, even when his method turned out to be slightly more complicated than that of most of the other surgeons. She found, to her unvoiced dismay, that when they were not rowing, she actively enjoyed being in this man's presence.

'Is that it?' Lucy looked askance down at her bruised ribcage and the surprising lack of major injury.

'That's it. I could do some running stitch down the middle, if you wanted it, young lady,' he laughed, 'but it wouldn't do anything for you.'

Louise covered up the girl and, hands still gloved, walked to the sink to rinse out a bowl. Giles followed her.

'Thank you, Sister. That was most efficient.' So

he had noticed that compatibility, too. It was the sort of thing that was valued highly in theatre, Louise knew. An alert, empathetic nurse could make a huge difference to the amount of strain the surgeon underwent.

'All in a day's work, Mr Levete,' she said dryly, and immediately regretted the coldness of the tone. Oh, it had become almost automatic these days! How practised she was, how able to deter and put down with every word!

'Always the same Sister Slater—so cool; so determined not to have to give anything.' He looked her firmly in the eye, and his dazzling blue gaze held something on the verge of pity, she thought. 'Would it have cost you so very much just to agree that we make a decent team?'

She was silent, aware of Lucy listening from the bed and of the trundling approach of the drinks trolley—and thus Nurse Rees. How she longed just to say that she *did* agree; that there was no offence meant; that for all he knew, she *did* have a heart. But it was impossible. Instead she pulled her eyes away from his and reached for the tap. But he caught her wrist before she could turn it, and, with a swift movement that even Lucy couldn't have seen, brought it to his lips, where he placed a light kiss at her pulse point, just where the plastic glove had folded down.

Her heart pounded wildly for a moment as emotions chased through her—profound shock to a system that had for so long been dedicated to the prevention of such an assault. Oh, she had been kissed by Mr Amery at Christmas. Mr Da Costa had pecked her on the cheek at the little party they'd held to celebrate his forthcoming marriage.

But to be caught unawares like this, for no reason . . .

For a moment Giles watched the confusion and sheer panic hit her. Felt her stiffen by his side and saw the blue eyes darken as if in thought—or pain. And then his lips began to sting slightly and the taste of antiseptic touched his tongue.

'Revenge is yours, Sister,' he muttered almost under his breath. 'I had no idea you prepared yourself for work by dabbing a little eau de sodium hypochlorite on each wrist. A cunning defence —and quite in character!'

And with a grimace, his nose wrinkling as the full force of the chemical Louise had used to swab Lucy's skin reached his taste-buds, he set off in search of Miss Osborne.

Louise stood at the sink and, quite without thought, turned on the taps. The adrenalin tearing through her system made her head ache wildly and a tiny area of her right wrist, just above the pulse point, spattered accidentally with Milton fluid and kissed for the first time in fifteen years, burned and burned.

CHAPTER FOUR

THE REST of the morning seemed to disappear in a kind of daze. Mr Levete had already examined Miss Osborne, pronounced her well enough to wait until her scheduled operation on Monday and signed two forms and a drugs authorisation before Louise returned to her office. Within, she found Rosie glowing, holding the papers to her ample bosom.

'He's such a charming man,' she told Louise, who was not in the frame of mind to believe the words. 'He's worked himself up into a real state about young Lucy, hasn't he? So fatherly . . .'

Louise decided that it was best to say nothing. If he had her nurses eating out of his hand, good for him. But as for her . . . Total confusion boiled within her. A vague sense of sickness competed with flashing sensual excitement, a feeling that she thought had been suppressed long ago. And on top of it all lay a thick layer of indignation that he should invade her privacy, mock her as he did. And yet, she was honest enough to acknowledge as she sat at her desk and mechanically filled out next week's duty roster, it had been her fault; if only she had found it within her to be polite, warm, generous to him when he'd commented that they made a good team. That's what any *normal* woman would have done. Normal. What did that mean? Was it normal to simper and flatter and bat eyelashes at men? Then perhaps she wasn't normal.

But in her situation, with a son and a responsible job, it wasn't really possible to lead a normal life, was it?

But what had happened to her that she could no longer appreciate a joke, a bit of friendly persiflage from a colleague? It wasn't that there was anything *wrong* with his attention. He was a married man, a professional, and his attempts at friendship had been the casual ones of a man secure in his marriage and his position. Nothing nasty, just jokey and deflating. If only she had played it that way too —then perhaps they might have developed the sort of relationship that the new Mrs Da Costa had had with Mr Morton and which Louise had watched and smiled at. They joked together, worked together, teased each other—but only to jolly things along. It didn't go deeper than that, did it?

A thought occurred, one so painful that she put down her pen for a moment and looked out of the window. Had she turned into a man-hater? Had she gone from being a woman who couldn't afford to let herself get involved with a man to one who wanted to hurt men; who blamed them for something outside herself? She'd given Mr Levete little enough chance to get to know her. And think how off-hand she'd been to Victor Inskip when he'd called with his invitation . . . She would have to think about the future very carefully, for it wouldn't be long before Dan left home, and when he did she'd find herself lonely and bored, with nothing but trips to her sister's and her Thursday keep-fit class to fill her life. Sometime soon she was going to have to start allowing people back into her life.

* * *

It was nearly six when she got home, for it had taken her an age to find a suitable dress for this evening in the shops. Louise opened the front door, allowed Cosmo to slide in around her legs, and wondered what on earth Dan was doing, cooking on a Saturday evening when he was normally more bothered with doing his hair and getting his trousers pressed.

'I'm home,' she called up the stairs, but there was no reply.

Leaving the dress bag in the hall, she followed the cat into the kitchen, curiosity overcoming her.

'Hello, Mrs Slater! I hope you don't mind me taking over your kitchen like this, but Dan and I are going to a concert in Hammersmith and we've got to leave before long. He wasn't going to have anything to eat after work, but I told him that after a day stacking shelves he'd need a proper dinner.' The vision that greeted Louise's eyes smiled and extended a hand in a rubber glove, then laughed and pulled it off. 'I'm Becca, by the way.'

Not only was Becca wonderfully down to earth about domestic matters and keeping Dan well fed, but she was also quite stunningly attractive. She stood at the sink, quite unselfconsciously scrubbing a saucepan, with her long, thick, wavy blonde hair cascading down her back, the remnants of a summer tan freckling her cheekbones and elegant nose and an infectious smile at the corners of her full mouth. She wore stylish white trousers that tapered above her ankles and flat blue pumps which showed off narrow feet and a well-turned leg, and several T-shirts, all managing to slip flatteringly from her shoulders, where glimpses of more tanned skin were exposed. In short, she was a fashionplate.

Young, vital, slightly provocative. And Dan was apparently going out with her.

Momentarily Louise felt a twinge of jealousy, for this girl was exactly the sort to take Dan away from her. But she covered it with an amused smile and accepted the offer of coffee that was immediately returned. Becca could even, she noticed, cope with the kettle-lid that usually had visitors to the house flummoxed.

'Have you had a hard day at work?' the girl asked easily as she got on with the washing-up.

'Not too bad.' Louise watched as each spoon was carefully placed in the drawer. 'Have you been working, Becca? Do you have a Saturday job?'

'I've only recently moved into the area, so I haven't had time to find one yet, but I expect I shall.' Again that dazzling smile, that air of complete confidence that only the young have. 'I think it's good to have a Saturday job, don't you? My father says there's no need, but it keeps you out of mischief—particularly the boys—and it gives you something you can call your own. Do you agree?'

'Oh, absolutely.' Louise murmured. Good lord, she hoped Dan realised that this girl had no stars in her eyes! But in a way she felt grateful that it was Becca who Dan was going out with tonight. He wouldn't get into much trouble with her around. As if on cue, Dan's feet came clattering down the stairs.

'Ah, Mum—you've met Rebecca, I see. You don't mind her cooking supper, do you? It's just that if we'd left it any later . . .'

'I don't mind at all!' Louise assured him. 'It's very nice to come home and find that I don't have to cook for you.'

'Oh, you *will* eat with us, won't you, Mrs Slater?
I'd reckoned on feeding three. Or if it's too early
yours can stay in the oven until you're ready for it.'
Becca looked concerned to think that she could
have cooked a meal and left Louise unfed. 'It's
nothing special, just lamb chops—'

'They're not out of the fridge, either,' Dan interrupted. 'Becca wouldn't hear of us coming in here
and eating your supplies, so I picked these up at
work.'

Speechless, Louise merely nodded. What
thoughtfulness! This girl really knew her way to a
parent's heart. And she could cook, too, if the
tender chops and surrounding vegetables were
anything to go by.

'Only fruit salad to follow, I'm afraid,' Becca
apologised. But what fruit salad—full of peaches
and strawberries and tiny grapes . . .

'That was wonderful! I hope you're going to
make a habit of this,' was all Louise could say when
she'd finished. 'I'll do the dishes—you two had
better be off.'

But no. Becca insisted that she and Dan do the
dishes too—and from Dan came not a squeak of
protest. Louise enjoyed another cup of coffee and
watched them at the sink, joking quietly and dis-
cussing the best route to the converted cinema in
which tonight's concert was to be held.

'You're not actually going to go next door
tonight, are you, Mum?' Dan asked incredulously
as Becca went to tidy up and Louise fetched in her
dress bag.

'I thought I would,' Louise admitted, feeling
suddenly as if their situations had been reversed.
She had been fed and cared for and now she was

being warned not to go out! 'Why shouldn't I?' she asked defiantly. It was a question she'd heard many a time from him!

Dan's face fell as he tried to work out the answer. 'Well—I didn't like him much when he came round. He was—well, you know . . .'

His troubled eyes studied her. 'I don't want you getting mixed up with someone like him,' he said at last, and he stroked her hand.

'For goodness' sake, I'm only going to a house-warming do! I'm perfectly able to look after myself, thank you, Dan. I shall be back here well before midnight, and I'll promise not to have more than two sherries if it'll make you feel any better!'

Dan's concern had flicked her on the raw because only yesterday she would have said exactly the same thing about Victor Inskip herself. But damn it—she'd bought a dress and worked herself up this afternoon to go next door and face him and their other neighbours, knowing all to well the difficulties a divorced woman faces in such circumstances.

'I was only trying to give you some advice. I wish I was going with you.'

'I'll be perfectly all right. You worry about me and I'll worry about you, okay? And we'll both have a terrible evening.' Louise leaned forward impulsively and pecked him on the cheek, noticing how clean he smelled, how newly-shaven; how like his father. And as if sensing her sadness, he suddenly hugged her to him for a few seconds, and they were close again, as they had been when he was a child.

'Go on—have a lovely time. And don't think twice about me.' Louise pulled away, something inside her telling her that it was up to her to be strong now, her turn to give him confidence. For a moment they rubbed noses in another childhood gesture of affection, and then Becca's footsteps as she came back from the cloakroom forced them apart.

'Well, do I look great—or do I look great?' Dan sprang to her side and twirled in a show-off fashion, giving them both a chance to admire his smart grey suit, cut long and lean and not at all, in Louise's opinion, the thing to wear to a concert.

'Me too!' Becca pirouetted at his side, now looking amazingly sexy in a bright red mini-dress cut on giant sweatshirt lines and red high heels.

'You both look terrific,' Louise laughed. They did—oh, how wonderful they looked, how confident and happy!

And still laughing and joking, she saw them to the door and waved them off before it occurred to her that Dan had been going with Martin—and like a true best friend, Martin had sacrificed his ticket for the cause of true love . . .

Clutching her glass of white wine as if it would stop her from drowning in the sea of chit-chat that rose and fell around the room, Louise allowed her eyes to take in Victor Inskip's sitting-room. He'd explained briefly as he'd greeted her in his habitual unctuous manner that he was an antique dealer —which was probably why the house was scattered with attractive, if slightly heavy and ornate, pieces of furniture. She sat now on an ornately carved Victorian sofa, hideously uncomfortable. Just opposite was the chaise longue that Dan had spotted being carried into the house—and indeed, it was very much like theirs.

'The twin to your own, except for the up-
holstery!' Victor settled himself at her side and
tried to pour more wine into her untouched glass.
'If you ever decide to get rid of it, I'd make you a
decent offer. Two hundred and fifty pounds, say—I
don't suppose you realised it was worth so much,
did you? That's what everybody tells me!'

'I wouldn't have put that price on it, no,' Louise
said quietly, aware that he'd edged a little closer
and that his thigh was touching hers. Well, perhaps
the man who'd valued it so highly when it had gone
to be re-upholstered hadn't *really* known what he
was talking about . . .

'I'm very angry with you, Louise.'

Her startled gaze and immediately icy eyes made
him laugh. 'Not really! But you haven't been en-
tirely honest with me, have you, my dear? I've just
heard from my other neighbours that you're divorced—not married to some ungrateful globe-
trotter, as I'd thought! Now what . . .' he edged
closer and ran his finger over the back of her hand
'. . . could have made you tell me such a thing?'

No matter how much she had determined to
leave Sister Slater at home in the closet with her
uniform, Louise was unable to stop the ice floating
to the surface of her voice.

'I don't think my marital status has anything to
do with you at all, Mr Inskip! The fact that I'm
divorced will not prevent me from keeping an eye
on your house when you're away on holiday or even
lending you the occasional cup of sugar. I'm not,
I'm afraid, one for believing that neighbours should
always be in and out of each other's homes.'

'You disappoint me, Louise.' Victor Inskip drew

away and regarded her with mocking eyes that weren't unlike a certain surgeon's. 'I'd thought that two divorced people—you see, I'm divorced too —would be able to understand each other better. After all, we've both been through the mill, haven't we? Neither of us is exactly—inexperienced, eh? And even if we'd neither of us want to get involved again, I had hoped we might be able to be more . . . friendly.'

He placed his hand firmly on her knee, and beneath that ultra-ordinary exterior and inoffensive appearance Louise noticed for the first time how calculating his eyes were—and how disgustingly complacent.

Louise toyed with several ideas. Phrases ran through her head. *You're the last man on earth I'd want to be friendly with*—well, that would be accurate. Or perhaps she should just throw her wine over him and storm out? But that would be folly. Even if she never saw the man again, he might make life difficult in all the niggly little ways that a neighbour can.

'I'm afraid you're too late,' was all she said. 'I already have other "arrangements".' Intentionally she borrowed his innuendo.

'Oh, well,' suddenly his whole countenance brightened as his fear of rebuff lifted, 'here's to you—and the lucky man!'

They were just toasting each other, Louise feeling guilty about her deceit but relieved at its effect, when Giles Levete was ushered into the room. At first he didn't recognise her, for with her hair down and waving gently about her face and a slim, cowl-necked sweater dress in a vibrant greeny-blue softly outlining her figure, she was a far remove from the sharp-edged, fanatically neat sister of Women's Surgical. And then suddenly the realisation of who she was, and with whom she was sitting, hit him. Irrational anger, the anger that seemed to consume him whenever he came into her presence, hit him too. He had come along, out of politeness and nothing more, to have a speedy drink, show his face and then retreat to his comfortable home and perhaps the late night film on TV. And here was Sister Slater, to irritate him yet again!

He provocatively eased his way between a couple of strangers and approached the pair on the hideous sofa. So long as Inskip saw his face and exchanged a few words, he couldn't feel put out that Giles wasn't prepared to stay longer.

'Ah, Doctor!' To Louise's relief, Victor's gaze moved from the outline of her breasts to the man who'd approached unnoticed. Her eyes followed her host's—and met the furious, stormy blue of Giles Levete's as he stood almost menacingly over them.

'This is Dr Levete, Louise. In fact I think he works in the same hospital as you, don't you, Doctor?' Inskip was all fulsome politeness again.

'*Mr*, actually. It's a fact not widely enough known that when one graduates to FRCS from the humble rank of doctor one becomes plain Mr again. Good evening, Sister Slater.' Giles nodded casually to Louise, who leaned back into the lumpy horsehair depths of the sofa and wished profoundly that she'd taken Dan's advice not to come out this evening. Could anything have been worse? Propositioned by her next-door neighbour and now with Mr Levete to face . . . What on earth was he doing here?

Deciding that neither surgeon nor nurse were very good company, Victor made an excuse and got up to go. Louise was relieved. Giles Levete might be difficult, but at least he was subtle and—well, she had to admit it—attractive. And being a married man and with his reputation to consider, he was most unlikely to cause a scene here.

'Hello,' she murmured nervously as he seated himself by her, unaware of the relief that shone for a second in her panicked eyes and turned them to an enchanting sea green. 'What are you doing here?'

'That's my line,' he laughed. 'I'm supposed to ask what a nice girl like you is doing in a place like this.'

'I live next door.' It was said with such rueful force of feeling, such certainty that it was only politeness that brought her here, that Giles felt something akin to surprise.

'At last, Sister, you and I have something in common. Because were it not for the fact that Victor Inskip sold me some furniture when I moved here and that it would have seemed rude to turn down the invitation, I wouldn't be here, either. Nasty little creep, isn't he?' His eyes flicked towards Victor, who was already chatting up another local lady, and Louise laughed with instant agreement.

'You probably didn't get much of a bargain in the furniture line, I'm afraid,' she told him. 'He's just offered to take something of mine off my hands for nearly half of what it's really worth.' She didn't mention the conversation he'd interrupted. 'Do you know many of the people here?'

'None at all.' Giles's gaze had turned to her,

taking in at closer quarters the way her hair, almost black, touched her cheek, and how her under-stated make-up brought out the almost sensual fullness of her lips and the length of her eyelashes. 'But to be frank, I'm not really interested in meet-ing them. I'm not one to get involved with my neighbours' lives, I'm afraid.' He noticed the way her fingers held the wine glass so tightly that her knuckles were quite white, the stiffness of her posture, the effort that talking to him cost her. And the anger that had been burning his heart subsided into amused protectiveness.

'You're here on your own, I take it?' he asked gently, stretching his legs so that she could take in the sheer length of them and the well-used grey corduroy trousers he wore—for he was very casu-ally dressed in black sloppy sweater and sports jacket.

'Yes.' She faltered. She didn't want any more advances. 'Dan already had something on.'

'I see.' Well, that was telling him, Giles decided. And good luck to Dan, whoever he was. It was obviously no use trying to talk about personal things, so he reverted to a subject they could dis-cuss without too much heat. Work. 'Did you hear about Lucy Higgins?' he tried, only to see her plunged into confusion, blushing and turning from him. Of course! He'd pecked her on the wrist and then been rude, hadn't he?

'I'm sorry about my behaviour this morning, Sister,' he added immediately. 'I had other things on my mind and I was most unprofessional.'

'You certainly were!' Louise allowed herself a little of Sister's coldness, then tried to maintain her out-of-work character. 'But what was this about

Lucy?' Interested, she turned and looked at him properly for the first time this evening—and noticed that that tiny spot of blood was still on his chin. He obviously hadn't had time to wash and shave.

'Apparently when the police at last got in to interview her, she admitted that she'd been involved with stealing a car and driving it away. She and a boyfriend. I couldn't believe it—a young girl like that . . .' He shook his head, then took a sip of his wine. 'Who would have thought it? Such a nice young girl.'

'It's a difficult age, isn't it,' Louise agreed, her thoughts suddenly with Dan and Becca. 'Even the nicest kids seem to tread on shaky ground. I suppose it's got something to do with growing up and trying out their wings—it's bound to result in a few problems.'

'It's frightening being a parent, though. I worry about my daughter all the time—all those young ruffians she hangs about with. You should see the way some of them look when they come to the front door—in fancy dress, almost . . .' Louise looked at his own well-worn clothes and thought of Dan's sharp suit. Perhaps Mr Levete's daughter was particularly outrageous—otherwise it looked like a case of the pot calling the kettle black!

'Perhaps you ought to lock her up,' she jokingly suggested. 'But it wouldn't do any good.'

'I know that, so I try to ensure that she can bring them home, give her as much freedom as possible so that she doesn't have anything to kick against—I try to show her I care for her, but it's difficult to talk to a girl that age at times.' He sighed, and Louise felt herself relax. At last he was human. At last they could talk without fighting, because, although he didn't know it, they both had the same problem.

'Can't your wife talk to her?' It was the obvious thing to ask.

Giles looked puzzled for a moment, then embarrassed as he contemplated his glass, and for a moment Louise realised she'd inadvertently stolen a march on him. 'I'm afraid my wife has her hands full with her new husband and step-family,' he said at last. 'It's partly because my daughter couldn't get along with her stepfather that she's come to live with me.'

'Oh, I see.' There was a long silence, full of complicated emotions. Louise felt surprised; a bit sorry for him; a sympathy with the problems he was going through, and a sudden dash of exhilaration, excitement mixed with fear, at the realisation that he was not quite the settled family man she'd thought. It explains his uncared for look, she thought, while Giles experienced all the embarrassment that came with admitting he'd had an unsuccessful marriage—and with the expressions of sympathy and, from the women, offers to look after him, that always followed.

I need time to get used to all this, Louise decided, glancing at her watch and discovering that it was all of half-past nine. The realisation that Giles Levete was not quite the safe ground she'd thought him worried her. She didn't want to start getting too friendly, did she?

'I must go,' she announced nervously and leapt immediately to her feet, catching him by surprise.

'I'll come too,' he insisted, and together, though apart, they waved goodbye to their host with insincere smiles and fought their way to the front door.

'Can I see you home?' Giles asked wryly as they escaped down the path. Louise wondered whether she ought to invite him in for coffee—but no. This 'new-woman' lark was getting out of hand. Sister Slater hadn't ever had a colleague from work back to her home for coffee or anything else. And Sister Slater would certainly not invite a scruffy, divorced, and none too reliable surgeon into her home.

'It's hardly necessary,' she heard herself say stiffly, and felt him recoil. For a few minutes they'd shared something, just as they'd shared something on the ward in their clashes. But that was going to have to be it; a brief, unsatisfying moment of something approaching sympathy. Because there was no room in either of their lives for further complications; no room for the protective barriers to come down.

'As you say, Sister.' That mocking tone was back in his voice. 'I'll wish you a good night.'

'Mr Levete? Stand still for a moment, will you?' As if in some way apologising for her briskness, Louise stood on tiptoe and, with the edge of her handkerchief, dislodged the speck of blood on his chin. The close contact of their bodies thrilled her for an instant, and she suddenly realised how provocative her action was—as if something inside her was driving her against her better judgment to seek his touch.

'There, that's better.' She stood back and gave a grimace which he took to be a nervous smile.

'Thank you, Sister.' Well, he had kissed her, and now she had had revenge by tidying him up as if he was a child, Giles decided as he strode off down the road, hands in his pockets. Even so, she was an attractive woman—and damned intriguing. Better than the other harpies who'd tried to attach themselves to him. Who was Dan, he wondered? Her husband? Something in the way she behaved persuaded him that she wasn't married. And she didn't wear a wedding ring, only a simple emerald on her ring finger. Engaged? Maybe. Then wasn't it quite mad to start thinking of inviting her out? And anyway, only a madman would want to get involved with an ice-woman like that . . .

Without realising what he was doing, Giles took a wrong turning and spent the next half-hour trying to find his way home.

CHAPTER FIVE

'YOU'RE quite welcome to stay to lunch, Becca —but won't your family be expecting you home?' Louise bustled round the kitchen, checking to see if the roast beef was done and hoping Dan had remembered to pour sherry for his aunt and uncle, whom he was entertaining in the sitting-room with stories of his adventures at last night's concert. That he got on well with her sister's family and that they provided the extra support needed was something for which Louise was eternally grateful. If anyone was like a father to him, it was her brother-in-law.

'Oh, it's all very free and easy at home,' Becca replied casually. 'I sometimes wonder whether my father actually gives a damn what I get up to!'

'I'm sure he *does*,' Louise felt shocked that the girl could think such a thing. Unless her father was a complete monster, of course. 'You'd be surprised what we parents go through, you know. And there's the constant problem of never knowing whether to be tough or lenient with you. He's obviously decided to give you a free hand; that shows he trusts you.'

'Big deal!' Becca stirred the gravy with a fork in one hand, and piled roast potatoes into a serving dish with another. 'You should hear the fuss he makes about my boyfriends coming to the house. He doesn't say they can't come, but he always goes on about how weird they look!'

Mindful of Giles Levete's words last night, and her own amused response to them, Louise said nothing on that subject. But, 'Well, if you want to call and let them know, you're welcome to use the telephone,' she offered. 'I wouldn't like to think of your lunch sitting on the table at home getting cold.'

'Oh, we don't usually have anything special,' Becca informed her airily. 'It's too much bother. But this looks wonderful—the first proper roast dinner I've had for ages.'

Louise shrugged a little—it sounded a very odd home set-up indeed to her—but reasoned that Becca was an eminently sensible girl and would know if a phone call *was* necessary. All the same . . .

Lunch passed off well. Dan and his cousins were bright and friendly to Becca and Louise enjoyed having a Sunday off. It wasn't such a rarity now that she was senior sister on her ward, but it was unusual enough for her to have a relaxing day just with her family. And all the adults were pleased to be spared the washing-up when, once again, Becca organised it.

'She's such a capable girl!' marvelled Louise's sister. 'Don't suppose you'd mind her for a daughter-in-law, would you?'

'Don't be ridiculous—Dan's just seventeen! I don't want him making the same mistakes I did,' Louise laughed. 'If he's not married at thirty I'm not going to be worried about it.' But the idea of Dan getting too involved with a girl as attractive and mature as Becca rankled. The very thought of a deep relationship with his other girlfriends had been laughable. They were all very young and very

silly and Dan had known it and treated them with
the light-hearted contempt they deserved. But in
the last couple of days he seemed to have grown up
quickly. Louise's mind went back to that brief
moment of closeness with him last night. There had
been something there, something new about him,
as if he'd realised something about himself—and
perhaps about her, too. He'd never given the slightest indication that he worried about her before . . .

Don't let him go falling in love, she thought
wildly, remembering what it had been like herself
at his age—the pain, the certainty that you knew it
all, and the terrible realisation that in actual fact
you knew nothing about life at all . . .

The day passed almost in a dream. They took
kites down to the heath and went for a long walk,
stopping for tea at one of the quaint tea-shops in
Highstead village, and then Becca and Dan went
back to her house, walking hand in hand, head to
head down the road, so patently falling for each
other that Louise's mouth went dry and she had
difficulty calling her goodbyes as she waved off her
sister and brother-in-law.

As she did the ironing in the kitchen that evening, all Dan's shirts waiting for her attention, she
tried to reason out why she should feel so fearful for
him. But it was difficult. Part of the problem lay in
the fact that in the last few days so much had
changed in her life. Two strangers had been intro-
duced into it, Becca and Giles Levete, and they'd
succeeded in upsetting all her plans, all her stable
routines. It was too bad of them. And yet though
they'd done little but cause chaos, Louise couldn't
honestly say, as she sprayed starch on to a limp
collar, that she wished they hadn't arrived. Dan

was entitled to a romance, and Becca was, as her sister had said, just the type of girl every mother hopes for for her son. And Giles Levete?

He was more difficult to think coolly about. But he'd shaken her out of a rut, hadn't he? And she should be grateful for that, at least. And if only he'd stop that terrible, mocking way of talking to her, he'd be nice, she told herself. Given time, they could have a good relationship on the ward. Perhaps, when the opportunity offered, she could tell him about her circumstances; tell him about Dan, let him know that he wasn't the only person in the world with such problems. What might his daughter be like? she wondered half-heartedly as she put a crease in Dan's jeans and then took it out again, remembering that at the moment she was under instructions to do so. Apparently it was out of fashion to be seen wearing jeans with a crease . . .

'Are all the admissions for theatre tomorrow present and correct?'

'Just the one to come in, Mrs Presfield, and she phoned and said there'd be a last-minute delay —couldn't get her domestic arrangements sorted out, apparently, and had to wait until her mother arrived to see to the kids,' Rosie explained.

'Good.' Louise ran her pencil down the checklist of things to do. 'Mrs Elsdon's gone down to Medical, I see, and Miss Callaghan was discharged as arranged. Hilton and Hooper due out tomorrow —thank goodness!' She raised a knowing eyebrow at her staff nurse and Rosie uttered an inaudible 'Hooray!'

'So that just leaves us with Miss Osborne in High

Dependency and the new intake to see to. It's nice to see a good turnover of patients, isn't it? Makes you feel as if you're being efficient.' Rosie reached for the notes that had been sent by the Records department for the newly admitted patients, and Louise and she went through them slowly, entering the relevant details on the Kardex.

'This one's a colostomy, so we'll get the stoma nurse in to see her this afternoon, if it's possible,' Louise decided. She was of the opinion that such an operation was more psychologically than physically damaging and tried to ensure that the patient knew all about her condition. So many doctors assumed that the procedures were too complicated and worrying for the patients to cope with, and preferred to keep them in the dark. Fortunately, Highstead was an enlightened place. There was a stoma nurse to help patients with colostomies and ileostomies, and a special adviser for women with gynaecological problems. It all ensured that a patient was as well prepared for life-changing surgery as possible.

'Gynae phoned while you were doing your round,' Rosie added. 'We'll be receiving two hysterectomies from theatre tomorrow morning. They'll be okay in Hooper and Hilton's beds, won't they?'

Louise marked the names on her ward plan. 'We'll have to play musical beds in our spare minutes tomorrow. Mrs Narasimhan will be staying by the nurses' station, but we'll have the new patients up this end, please.'

Rosie nodded and went off to see what she could do for one of the housemen who'd just called in. Louise continued checking, going through the notes so that nothing was missed. Giles Levete's first patients would be coming in over the next couple of days. He had a lobectomy tomorrow and two explorations—probably for lung cancer, though no one would know for certain until the ops were completed. Such cases put an emotional strain on the ward. It was difficult for the nurses to cope with the most difficult, terminal cases. And lung cancer, usually self-inflicted through smoking, aroused strong reactions from everyone.

On her notepad, Louise pencilled in a reminder to catch Mr Levete when he came to check his patients after visiting hours were over. The simple act of writing his name gave her a thrilled little feeling—the sort of feeling she'd known twenty years ago, writing Tony's name on her school pencil case—or even, daringly, *Louise loves Tony* on the toilet wall. A flood of embarrassment brought her mind back to the present. She'd just check with Mr Levete about the details of his patient's care; what drugs he wanted used, any particular likes, that sort of thing. Of course, he might see it as officious fussing, in the way he seemed to interpret almost everything she did—but at least he couldn't complain he hadn't been consulted about his patients and their care.

'Has Mr Amery explained to you what we'll be doing tomorrow?'

The woman in the bed looked fearful and Louise gently swished the curtain closed, hiding them from the prying eyes of Lucy Higgins—for Lucy had turned out to be 'a right handful—a real little madam', in Naomi Bryant's forthright words, and she liked to be in on everything.

'All I want to do, Mrs Aitken, is to ensure that

nothing that happens to you comes as a surprise —and to reassure you that however bad things seem now, you're going to get over them.'

'Oh, Sister! I don't know how I'm going to live with it! I wish it was so serious that they couldn't do anything for me, I really do . . .' Mrs Aitken broke down in a welter of sobs.

'Now that's silly,' Louise said sternly, but putting her arm round the patient to comfort her. 'In two weeks you'll be out of here—and though I don't promise that things will be just as they are now, you'll find life can go on as fully as before. *Better* than before! Think how miserable the colitis has made you.'

The stoma nurse had been unavailable, so Louise herself had taken the time to visit her colostomy patient and chat things over. 'What is it you're so frightened about, Mrs Aitken? Is it the operation itself?'

'No, after.' The woman dried her tears on a tissue and looked up. 'How on earth can I go out after that? It'll be so embarrassing . . .'

'No one will know unless you tell them.' From the white plastic box she'd brought with her, Louise withdrew the paraphernalia needed after a colostomy—after an artificial opening to the lower abdomen had been created to allow the exit of waste materials. Mrs Aitken had newly developed cancer of the colon after years of misery with colitis. This operation was a great blow, certainly —but she'd probably find her day to day activities easier with the bag Louise held on her palm fitted than she had for some time.

'Well, that's it. It's dreadful, isn't it?' she said in ironic tones, and smiled encouragingly. 'They'll insert an attachment at the opening and the bag connects to that, flat against your stomach. No one will ever guess you're wearing it. Once the operation's been done you'll be supervised by a special nurse who'll come in daily to show you what to do and how to look after yourself. Tell me—what did you think it was going to be like?'

Mrs Aitken said nothing for a moment, then slowly reached for the bag and handled it suspiciously. 'I thought it would look bigger—but this is quite small, isn't it?' she murmured. 'But how can I be sure that it's—well, that it's safe?'

'It *is*. I can tell you that until my face turns blue, of course, but when you've tried it out for yourself, with all the modern adhesives and materials available these days, you'll find that there's nothing to worry about.' There was a pause for a few moments and the patient put the bag back into the box, took a look at the other bits and pieces inside it, and then sat back. She didn't look exactly happy, Louise admitted—but then, what had she expected?

'How about your husband? How does he feel?' It was a difficult question to ask, but in cases like this a husband was often affected almost as profoundly as his wife. He bore the brunt of her moods and depression if she was unhappy. He'd supported her so far. And sometimes it was impossible for the couple to ask the sort of intimate questions that *really* concerned them, so while the wife discovered things as they happened to her, he was left in the dark.

'He wants me well again, of course,' Mrs Aitken admitted grudgingly. 'But—well, he's frightened, isn't he? As far as he's concerned, it's the end of . . . you know.' She glanced down at the sheets.

'If you mean the end of your married life, you're quite wrong,' Louise smiled, unembarrassed. 'You'll feel better, less drained, and there's absolutely no reason why you shouldn't go on with everything you've been doing.'

'Oh yes? With this?' Mrs Aitken caught up the appliance and held it up. 'How would your husband feel, Sister?'

'Well—' Louise thought quickly. It would be unduly complicated to admit that she didn't have a husband . . . 'well, I hope he'd be pleased that I was alive to be with him. And I'd also hope he loved me and cared enough for me to understand what was happening and try to help me through it.'

'And he wouldn't be put off by the fact that you were attached to one of these? Your husband must be an absolute saint, Sister—that's all I can say!' Mrs Aitken's voice had risen in pitch and volume and Louise realised that she was even more distraught than she'd imagined.

'It's all right, my dear—'

'I really don't know if you understand what ordinary people have to go through, you nurses,' Mrs Aitken barged on as Louise put away the white box and poured a glass of water for her. 'As far as I'm concerned, and my husband too, it'll mean the end of our marriage—our proper marriage . . .'

Louise sat purposefully at the edge of the bed and held out the glass. 'Here, have a sip of this and try to control yourself, Mrs—' she tried firmly, but Mrs Aitken had begun to cry uncontrollably again. At that moment the curtains parted and Giles Levete's leonine head appeared between them.

'Problem, Sister?' His voice was calm, quiet, and

he gazed with concern at the almost hysterical patient.

'I think perhaps a mild sedative would help Mrs Aitken. She's worked herself up—'

'Worked myself up? What can you possibly know? You and your saintly husband . . .' Tears overcame her again. Vague, muttered words surfaced every now and then, mostly about nurses being inhuman and not knowing how their interference with the human body ruined people's lives, but neither surgeon nor nurse took any notice. Giles quickly scanned the notes, suggested a drug to Louise, and, when she nodded assent, wrote it on the chart.

'I'll send one of your nurses down with it, Sister,' he promised calmly and was about to leave when Louise called him back.

'Mr Levete! Can I see you in my office in a few minutes? Just to discuss your patients,' she added as an afterthought as the glint in his eyes appeared again. He looked tired, she thought. And he certainly wasn't in the mood for hanging round hysterical patients.

Sure enough, Jenny Rees soon arrived with the tray carrying hypodermic syringe and an ampoule of the prescribed drug. Though she nearly upset the whole lot on to the floor, Louise had enough basic confidence in Jenny to allow her to administer the injection to an almost oblivious Mrs Aitken and then to stay by her side until she fell asleep.

Louise herself walked swiftly back up the ward, pausing to reassure one or two patients who'd been upset by the commotion that nothing was wrong. But sedating a patient always rankled. It was an acknowledgement that care and concern weren't enough. Louise wondered for a second whether she had been right to try to talk to Mrs Aitken—and whether she'd been sympathetic enough. After all, she *didn't* have a husband, and she wasn't going off to theatre tomorrow for major surgery . . .

'All right, Sister?' Giles caught her worried frown as she entered the office.

'Just asking myself if I'd done the right thing,' Louise admitted. 'Perhaps I should have left well alone.'

'What an admission! Can I have that in writing?' His sarcasm didn't sink in to her, and he realised that she really was troubled. 'Of course you did the right thing, Sister. Sometimes the facts are hard to take, but ignorance is never bliss.' He ran his hand through his hair and sat down heavily in the chair opposite her desk. 'Actually, that's something I wanted to talk about. One of the cases coming in for investigation on Wednesday looks inoperable to me, and I want you to help me decide when and how to break the news to her.'

Louise looked up suddenly and found him watching her carefully. All the sarcasm and humour had gone. In its place was calm professional interest. 'You'll know your own patient best,' she insisted. 'And if it's anything like this afternoon's outburst, I don't want to be there to see her reaction when you break the news.'

'You're going to take this all wrong, Louise, but I'm really pleased it bothers you.' That old gleam was there, somewhere, in his eyes and in the slight tremor of his lips. 'I really had begun to think that nothing moved you—that you were impervious to everything going on around you.'

She could think of nothing to say. How could she

explain that she tried purposely to ensure there
were no upsets, no histrionics, so that she could
keep her life on an even emotional keel? Mrs
Aitken's outburst had raised all the self-doubt, the
sense of something missing in her life, that she
could normally ignore.

'You're wrong, Mr Levete,' was all she said. 'I
just don't feel that I can give everything that's
required to my patients if the ward is in uproar and
my nurses racing everywhere. So I plan ahead. To
you it may seem fussy, but to me it's good sense.'

'I want you to talk to Mrs Hodge when she comes
in, try to see how she ticks, find out how
strong she is. I'm a great believer, Sister, in telling
people the truth—but if she can't take it, we'll have
to find some other way around the problem.'

'Most terminal cases guess, in my experience.
They seem to know. But I'll certainly do what you
ask,' she agreed. It was really no more than she'd
do anyway, Louise thought privately to herself.
Hadn't she got most of her patients summed up
already?

Quickly they ran over the cases to be nursed on
the ward in the next few days. Giles was not against
morphia—in fact he'd be interested in ex-
perimenting with some new pain-control ideas he'd
come across recently in which the patient con-
trolled the amount and regularity of her pain
control through a drip system. Louise bit her
tongue and didn't snap back that it sounded like
more trouble for the nurses—and it suddenly occurred to her that a few days ago Mr Levete would
most certainly have heard her opinion . . . He
wanted patients out of bed as soon as possible, but
he would exercise judgment. 'I trust you, of course,

Sister—you've seen more cases than I have. But I'll be doing a round every couple of days . . .'

Louise was surprised. Normally consultants came round a couple of times a week at the most. This one was certainly dedicated—or just enthusiastic! They finished the notes and he sat back and stuck his feet out in front of him—and for the first time, Louise noticed that they were bare.

'Where on earth are your shoes?' she asked incredulously.

'Your staff nurse noticed that they were rather muddy, so she took them away to clean them.'

'You mean Rosie . . . ? I'm sure she had better things to do—'

'I thought it was very kind of her to offer, actually. She's a good, motherly sort, Nurse Simpson, isn't she?' he asked provocatively, watching the muscles twitch in Louise's cheeks as she contemplated the sheer audacity of the man.

'Too kind-hearted by half! I won't have you taking advantage of her, Mr Levete,' she fumed.

'I didn't even ask!' His smug face across the table suddenly creased in smiles that emphasised the bags under his eyes. 'Will you do me a favour, Sister?'

'You can try asking,' Louise murmured grudgingly, wondering what back-handed compliment or head-on rebuke she was going to get now. The man seemed, despite all his assertions, to have something against ordinary straight talking. He approached everything in such a roundabout fashion—it was most confusing!

'Come out to dinner with me, will you? Leave Dan behind for the evening—'

'I'm afraid that isn't possible.' Just when she

thought her old barriers were beginning to crumble, he had made the fatal mistake of advancing too far. Immediately Louise was on the defensive. Not only that, she was furious with herself for having allowed him to get so far into her territory. For a few hours she'd actually begun to think quite warmly of him, to wonder about him and his life . . . But no good could come of getting close to someone like him. He'd not want a woman with a young ruffian to support; perhaps he was like Victor Inskip and saw her as an experienced, easy conquest . . .

The afternoon was ruined. Louise slammed all her careful notes into her drawer for filing later and refused to look at him as her self-reproach burned. Oh, how weak she'd been!

'I wanted to discuss the problems I'm having with my daughter with you. You seemed interested —even sympathetic. In fact, Sister, I thought over what you said quite carefully, and I think you're right. But we . . .'

'*We* nothing, Mr Levete. I was simply making polite conversation, that's all. And what I know about child-rearing could be written on the back of a postage stamp,' she lied. Giles watched her bristling and wondered what he could possibly have done to merit such a reaction. Could a grown woman, a woman as attractive as Louise Slater, be so easily upset by a simple request for dinner? She really seemed quite cut up. What on earth could have happened to her to make her like this?

'Okay,' he said mildly, where a week ago he would have made a flippant remark about the fact that he *had* planned to ravish her under the table during the main course, and she was wise to refuse the invitation. Something inside him told him she wasn't in the mood to take such a sarcastic gibe. She wouldn't be worn down by them; she'd just build her defences higher. 'I'm sorry I've upset you. I hadn't realised you were so strongly against staff fraternisation. Do you think Nurse Simpson would know anything about children?'

'I'm sure she'd be most sympathetic and constructive,' Louise said briskly, not daring to look at him for fear of what she'd see there. Because if he gave her one of the roguish smiles he sometimes used, she wasn't sure she could resist him, so difficult was the role of Sister Slater becoming these days. 'Why don't you ask her yourself—I see she's finished cleaning your shoes.' And she marched stiffly from the office, around the bulk of a bemused Rosie Simpson who'd just entered.

Giles couldn't resist the challenge. 'What are you doing tonight, Nurse? You see, I'm having problems with my teenage daughter, and I need some sensible female advice . . .'

From her dug-out in the nurses' station, Louise heard Rosie's delighted voice expressing enthusiasm and then arranging a time and place. Damn it; damn him; damn everything, she thought miserably as she ripped open the door of the medicine trolley and one hinge came flying off. Tonight she would go home and soak in a cold bath. And tomorrow the old ice-cool Sister Slater would stalk the wards once again!

The first sight that met her eyes as she let herself into the house that evening was of Becca standing at the turn of the stairs, leaning out over the banisters to Dan, who was trying to climb up.

'O, speak again, bright angel . . .'

'What on earth is going on?' Louise asked loudly.

'O Romeo, Romeo—your mother's just arrived!' Becca almost fell down the stairs laughing. 'Oh, Mrs Slater—you must think we're mad!'

'What's new?' Louise found herself laughing with them, though she wasn't aware of the joke.

'You're not going to believe it, Mum,' Dan jumped from the banisters, 'but we're Romeo and Juliet in the school play. A pair of star-crossed lovers if ever there was one. Don't you think it's romantic?' He kissed Becca gently on the lips and she placed a familiar arm around his waist. Louise watched—and wondered just how well they knew each other, and what she should say.

'It's great,' she managed without hesitation. 'Will we have the pleasure of seeing you in tights, Dan? I've got a lovely pair of red woolly ones that are too long in the leg for me. Do you a treat, though.'

'You'd look wonderful darling,' Becca teased.

'Alas, the world will be denied that particular thrill.' Dan made an elegant leg. 'I'm afraid it's all black leather and *West Side Story* sort of thing.'

'I like a nice musical,' Louise laughed, taking off her coat. Dan, ever chivalrous in front of his girl-friend, took it for her.

'No music, I'm afraid, Mum. But don't you think we'll make the perfect pair?' He kissed Becca again, more slowly.

'Just remember that in the play they both end up killing themselves,' Louise said wryly as she disappeared into the kitchen.

*   *   *

At the Cherry Tree, a smart pub-restaurant on Highstead Hill, Giles was trying to keep his mind on the ebullient Rosie and all she had to tell him about the traumas of growing up. He felt impossibly guilty for bringing her out on such false pretences. He could tell from the new flowery smock dress which billowed about her more than generous curves that she'd pulled out all the stops for him. He'd already complimented her on her hair, smiled broadly at her jokes, which were really very good. So why couldn't he concentrate on her very sound advice on how to bring up a teenage girl?

'I used to be a bit of a tearaway,' she admitted with a coy glance. 'I would be still if I got the opportunity.'

Giles blinked and realised a response was required. 'Oh, I can't believe you don't get lots of invitations to get up to something naughty,' he obliged.

'Plenty of invitations,' she nodded, 'but all from elderly gents on Men's Surgical who'd run for their lives if I said yes!'

Giles made all the right moves, everything automatically, but his heart and most of his mind weren't with his companion.

'Tell me,' he interrupted Rosie's account of her first attempt to run away from home, 'what do you know about Sister Slater?'

Rosie's smile faded. She'd been trying hard all evening to ignore the fact that every pore of Giles Levete's body emanated indifference to her presence. 'Nothing really,' she said flatly, feeling disappointment welling at another fairytale evening going wrong. 'She's a bit of a mystery.'

'Does she have a family?' Giles hated himself for pressing on in the face of such hurt, but he had to know. Louise was a puzzle, nagging away at him, refusing to be put aside.

'She used to live with her mother, I heard. She died not so long ago—we only knew about her because she had to come into hospital. But you know what they say—someone like her is bound to have a juicy secret stashed away.'

'Mmmm.' Giles glanced pointedly at his watch and Rosie, defeated, promptly rose to her feet.

'I must go—I'm working an early tomorrow.'

'I'll see you home,' he insisted mildly, and she did not say no, even though she knew it was all downhill from here—all embarrassed shuffling on the doorstep of the house she shared with four other nurses. All tears once she had bid him good-bye. But strangely enough, tonight it wasn't. For Giles kissed her with contrite tenderness and wished he could feel something more for such a kind, good-hearted woman. What had looks to do with it? Why did Louise, so strange, so cool, have to capture his imagination when this friendly, warm, ample creature could not?

'I haven't been a very good companion, Rosie,' he said gently. 'I'm afraid my mind's been on too many things this evening, and not all of them involving you. Forgive me, will you?'

Rosie was still quite shaken by the effects of his kiss, the unexpected warmth of his farewell.

'There's nothing to forgive,' she responded generously. 'It's been one of the loveliest evenings I've ever had. Would you like to come in for coffee?'

'No, not tonight.' Giles excused himself, and

turned down the garden path after watching Rosie enter the house.

'I'm in love,' she announced to an astounded flatmate making cocoa in the kitchen. 'Make me some, will you—because love always makes me hungry!'

Giles walked up the hill. It was more than a mile home, but he needed time to think—to ponder what Rosie had said about Louise. What was it about her? What could it be? What *was* Sister Slater's secret?

CHAPTER SIX

FOR THE hundredth time, Rosie approached the
gate to Sister's house, hesitated, and walked on,
coming to a faltering halt outside Victor Inskip's
home. She wished she'd never thought of the idea
of coming here in the first place, she decided miserably. In her hand, hot and sticky from nerves, was a
plastic carrier bag containing Sister's navy cardigan
which she had left in the office. It had seemed to
provide the obvious excuse—a chance to go round
to Sister's house and find out whether she really did
have a secret. Perhaps she was living with someone;
perhaps she was married . . . Whatever, if Sister
were to be removed from Giles Levete's thoughts
he might have some time for her, Rosie. It had
seemed such a brilliant idea only an hour or two
ago, but now it felt mean and sneaky and she
couldn't bring herself to do the dreadful deed.

With renewed resolve, she walked rapidly up the
garden path and planted one stumpy finger on the
bellpush before her conscience could deter her yet
again. If only Giles's kiss the other night hadn't
been so kind, so gentle, so caring, she wouldn't
have fallen hook, line and sinker for him—and
she wouldn't be here now.

'Hello.' Dan, who'd been busy learning lines
with Becca, tried not to sound too surprised when
he opened the door to Rosie's considerable bulk on
the doorstep. It was obvious by her uniform that
she was a nurse.

'Have you come to see Mum? I'm afraid she's out shopping at the moment.'

'Your Mum?' Rosie was flummoxed. She certainly hadn't expected the door to be opened by this flaxen-haired young man. 'Is Sister Slater your Mum?' she asked incredulously. Surely she wasn't old enough to have a son this age? And she'd certainly never mentioned him!

'Yes . . .' Dan's tone was hesitant. He wondered whether he'd said something he shouldn't have. 'Would you like to come in for a cup of coffee? You can wait for her—she won't be long. Is it something urgent to do with the hospital?'

Becca's face appeared behind him in the doorway. 'I can go and make a fresh pot of tea if you'd like,' she offered. Rosie continued to stand, bewildered, on the doorstep, the carrier bag clutched to her capacious bosom.

'Shall I tell Mum that you called?' Dan tried again, casting an anxious glance over his shoulder. Becca shrugged noncommittally.

'No, there's no need for me to come in.' As if woken from a dream, Rosie suddenly came to life. 'I only came to give your Mum her cardigan. She left it on the ward this afternoon and I thought she might need it. You're going away on holiday, aren't you?'

'Yes, to Yorkshire. Just for a few days.' Dan took the bag and looked inside. 'Well . . . Mum'll be very grateful for this, I'm sure. Who shall I tell her called? She'll want to know, so that she can thank you.'

'Tell her Rosie popped round—and that I hope she has a happy holiday.' With an unaccustomed spring in her step, Rosie took off down the path.

Sister Slater did have a secret after all. And now it was a secret no longer. If Sister had a son then she must have a husband too. And if she had a husband she couldn't get involved with Giles Levete. So joyous were her thoughts that Rosie bumped into Victor Inskip as he got out of his car, parked at the kerb.

'Hello there! It's nice to see someone happy about something,' he drawled in his ingratiating way. And Rosie stopped for a few moments to pass the time of day with him . . .

'*Rosie* called?' Louise couldn't hide her astonishment. 'What on earth did she think she was doing, coming here?' Dan handed her the cardigan, shrugging his shoulders.

'She said you'd left that behind at work and that you might need it for your holiday.'

'She did seem a bit—well, odd,' Becca added.

'She's gone completely mad, if you ask me,' Louise muttered. 'I wear navy blue all week at work and the girl thinks I want to use this on holiday! It's not as if I haven't left it in the office before, either. She didn't say anything else?'

'I suppose she was a bit surprised to see me.' Dan brought the last suitcase downstairs, nearly tripping over Becca, who was organising the wellington boots in the hall.

'I bet she was!' Louise's heartfelt exclamation went over the heads of the two youngsters. Rosie was too nice a girl to have come to call with anything but good intentions, but even so, Louise hated the idea that her home life was going to be public knowledge from now on. By the time she got back from Yorkshire the news that she had a family would be all over the hospital. Then her reign as ice queen of Women's Surgical would be over, for part of her success had been the aura of mystery that surrounded her. From now on she'd be classified just like any other working mother, not the sort of higher mortal she appeared to be at the moment.

For some inexplicable reason she felt inclined to blame the whole thing on Giles Levete. The rot had set in on the very day he had arrived and made such a fool of her by massaging her bad back. Something very worrying had begun to happen then, something she wasn't quite able to understand. Well, at least she'd have a few days' peace away from him in Yorkshire with her sister and brother-in-law and Dan. It was a pity that Becca's father had refused her permission to come too—but then, from what she'd heard, Louise thought that Becca's father sounded a very unreasonable sort of man.

The hooting of a car outside alerted them to the fact that the rest of the family in their estate car had arrived. They would take the bulk of the luggage and leave Dan and Louise to follow in Louise's old Mini. As Dan kissed Becca a fond farewell and helped to load everything into the two cars, all thoughts of Rosie and Giles fled from Louise's mind.

'*Sister?* Never! You got the wrong house, Rosie!' Carolyn took another gulp of her coffee and moved along as Jenny Rees joined them.

'I'm telling you—she has a son. He must be about sixteen and he looks just like her! I'm not having you on, Carolyn! He told me she was his Mum.'

'What about her husband? Isn't he around?

Sister's such a conventional sort of character I can't imagine her . . . Well, you know.'

'He wasn't there when I called, but I bumped into the chap who lives next door and he told me that she's divorced. I got the feeling he was rather interested in her himself.' Rosie blushed so promptly that Jenny couldn't but ask why. 'Well, he asked me to go out for a drink with him one evening,' Rosie confessed. She didn't tell them that she didn't like the look of Victor Inskip half as much as she did Giles Levete—there was no point in that.

'It must be a tough life for her, having a son to look after and having to keep us organised as well,' Carolyn mused. 'No wonder she's such a tartar at times. Can you blame her for keeping everything on a tight rein?'

'Who's keeping who on a tight rein?' Tracy Furlow, from Men's Medical, sat down at the table. 'Come on, you lot! What's the hot news? Have you heard that Walsh and Slater are planning to ask for ward clerks? The rumour is that it'll mean one less nurse is needed on each of the wards. We must plan our response!'

And so news of Sister Slater's secret began its insidious spread across the hospital; from the nurses' canteen it went to the young doctors, many of whom lived in considerable fear of Louise and rather enjoyed the proof that she was human after all. And from them it passed to the highest echelons of the hospital, to the kitchens, to the auxiliaries, to the patients—and, finally, to Giles Levete.

'My dear Sister Slater—you have been deceiving me all this time.' Giles sat confidently on her desk, one long leg swinging casually over the wastepaper basket, watching discomfort wash over Louise like a wave.

'Really, Mr Levete? And how might I have done that?' Her tartness was sheer bravado—in reality she was unsettled by the amusement and confidence in his eyes and hovering about his sensual lips.

'You persuaded me that there was a man in your life and that you knew nothing at all about teenagers—so I suppose, in a way, that you've deceived me twice!'

His face expressed laughing reproach, as if he was ticking off a badly-behaved child who amused him. 'In fact, Sister, you told me that what you knew about child-rearing could be written on the back of a postage stamp—and that patently isn't correct, if what I've heard about your young Adonis of a son is true.'

'What have you heard about Dan?' she asked quickly. Rumour about herself was one thing, about Dan another.

'Oh, that he's the best-looking teenager in the whole of north London, with impeccable manners and excellent dress sense. In fact I'd like to meet him myself; he sounds too good to be true! Nothing like the load of teenage oafs my daughter hangs about with.'

Dan, magnified by rumour, did sound too good to be true, Louise thought wryly. If only Giles Levete and Rosie Simpson really knew!

'I'm sorry if I've confused you,' she said carefully. 'I like to keep my private life and my work separate. As you know yourself, it's not easy.'

His eyes caught hers and she glimpsed in them

understanding, sympathy—admiration, even—
and she couldn't help but warm to him, difficult,
mocking though he was. Why had she been so harsh
to him? After all, he was suffering the same problems, worse by the sound of it, that she was. If they
shared their experience of child-raising it might
halve the burden on each of them.

'Are they giving you a hard time?' He motioned
out to the ward and the knowing looks and raised
eyebrows Louise had been receiving all morning.

She smiled at his perceptiveness. 'I suppose it's a
revelation to them. They all thought I was a thorny
old spinster with my knitting and my cat to go back
to each evening.' Her laugh held the slightest trace
of bitterness. 'If only they knew what it was really
like.' She said it quietly, with feeling.

'I do. It's a cruel world, being left on your own to
cope. And people start to behave very oddly when
they hear you're divorced, as if there's something
terrible wrong with you. You've done very well for
yourself, Louise. Come a long way on your own.'

There was a long silence, with only the slight
swish of his leg as he swung it over the top of the
wastepaper basket. Louise watched the scuffed toe
of his shoe and understood what had motivated
Rosie to offer to clean his brown brogues the other
week. There was something comforting but also
vulnerable about the man; he was strong but he also
had something missing from him; there was a depth
to him that hid a deeper emptiness, she knew
instinctively. It was something she had felt in herself. She was older, wiser, but very much sadder for
what had happened to her.

'We're two of a kind, Sister. So how about
coming out for a drink with me and really giving the

vultures out there something to talk about? Come and tell me how to look after my daughter, and I'll teach you the rules of cricket or something, so that you can impress your son.'

'I already know the rules of cricket,' Louise replied defiantly, watching that gleam in his eye. 'Do you know about the latest pop fad? About Boy George?'

'Lord no! I'm above things like that,' Giles exclaimed, pressing a melodramatic hand to his brow.

'Well, that's the problem then. I used to wear a mini skirt and stay out late myself, you see, Mr Levete, so I have some sympathy for your daughter,' she smiled. Should she go out with him, even for a drink? It would be bound to be noticed by someone; even if they went to Land's End there would be bound to be a Highstead nurse holidaying there to note everything they said and did. But what did it matter? Now that the old Sister Slater was well and truly exposed as a fraud, who cared?

'Come for a drink, Louise, and tell me all about it.' He was serious now, intent. 'I need your help and advice and support. I've said some silly things to you before now, but that was because I've felt that we've had something in common all the time. Now I'm proved right, I hope I won't have to keep chipping away at you. I know what it is and I understand. Who knows, perhaps I can help you—though you seem to have everything sorted out perfectly anyway.'

'Well . . .' It was a major decision for her, one which might change her life.

'Please, help a father in distress! I don't know where my daughter *is* half the time, and there's nothing I can do that doesn't annoy her and make her more difficult. I need a mother's advice.'

'What about her mother, can't she—' Louise drew away from him again.

'Sister, Mr Amery is here for his round.' Rosie's flushed face appeared round the door and took in the casual closeness of the consultant and the senior nurse with a desperate sweep of the room.

'I'd better come. We're still having bother with Mrs Aitken and I want a word with him about her. Mr Levete, excuse me, will you?'

She got up to go, a strange feeling of disappointment that she'd been unable to accept his request for advice thudding in her.

'Louise?' His eyes said what he didn't want to express in front of Rosie's wagging ears. She paused, picked up Mrs Aitken's case notes.

'All right. Let me know when and where.' And with a meaningful nod she went off in search of Mr Amery.

Rosie watched a slow smile spread across Giles' face and swallowed the tears fighting to escape.

'Hello there, Rosie,' he said warmly as he followed in Sister's wake. But the warmth was not for her, she knew. Not for a fat nurse who talked too much and fell in love too easily, but for a mature, attractive woman whose heart he'd discerned long ago under a thick layer of ice.

The Flying Horse was one of Highstead's most popular wine bars. It had a long front counter for those who'd just come to drink and a cosy, intimate and relaxed back area where decent food was available. It was also regularly packed out with staff from the hospital and tonight was no exception.

Heads were raised and eyebrows with them as Giles
Levete ushered a trembling Louise through the bar
to the table he'd reserved at the back. The conversation at one table, occupied, as luck would
have it, by Rosie and two of her flatmates, came to
an abrupt halt as the couple passed.

'Hello, Sister,' Rosie tried in a dulled voice, but
Louise was too nervous to have noticed and sailed
blithely past, intent on having a drink and getting
away as soon as possible. Rosie fumbled in her
handbag for her handkerchief and her two companions eyed Giles as if he were some sort of pervert,
upsetting their friend like this.

'What will you have?' Giles peered over the top
of his menu and noticed the way Louise's vibrated
gently and how white her fingertips were.

'I'm not hungry, really,' she began. 'Perhaps we
could just have a drink and then go home?'

Giles's eyebrows rose. 'Well *I'm* starving,
Louise. And I didn't book a table and bring you
down here for a quick drink.' He smiled reassur-
ingly at her and rubbed the backs of the fingers
which held her menu with his own index finger.
'Relax. I want you to have a pleasant evening,
that's all.'

'I'm not used to going out—not with . . .' Her
face glowed with confusion. How could she tell him
that, apart from a few ruinous dates when she'd first
started her training and the odd meal out with her
family, she'd not been out to dinner with a man for
ten years? It was a ridiculous thing for a woman her
age to admit to! And he'd never understand why
she was so nervous—why all these familiar faces
staring at her made her want to shrivel up and die.
In her uniform, in her official capacity, she could

face them, but what had happened to her that she couldn't face them as plain, simple Louise Slater?

'You're not used to going out with a man or you're not used to going out, full stop? Which is it?' Giles's bright blue eyes seemed unperturbed, not even, for once, amused. Just probing.

'Both,' she admitted shamefacedly. 'I'm afraid you'll find me very boring. I've lost the art of social chit-chat.'

'We didn't come here to make small talk,' he reminded her. 'And simply because you haven't had a hectic social life recently doesn't make you boring, Louise.'

His charming approach, far from putting her at her ease, simply made her all the more suspicious. It was difficult to believe he was the same man as the sardonic surgeon who seemed to take delight in belittling her at work. But was her suspicion rightly grounded, or was it merely habit? His smile, lighting up his face, persuaded her for a moment that his interest was genuine. He was so handsome, so maturely attractive in a craggy, honest sort of way that she couldn't bring herself to accept her worst imaginings. It was crazy to trust him—but what choice did she have?

'Does your son have a girlfriend?' he asked casually.

'Oh yes! She practically lives with us,' Louise laughed, 'but I don't suppose it will last for long. He gets very involved in things and people, then tires of them. It's all part of being young, I suppose.' Her thoughts turned to her past; to Tony. Had it just been youthful obsession, mistaken for love, that had thrown them so disastrously into marriage? If she was going to be honest, Louise admitted wryly that it probably was. How could you know what love really was at seventeen?

'So you reckon she'll grow out of it—all this anti-social behaviour?'

'If you keep her roughly on the straight and narrow, I think she will,' she said cautiously. 'Just don't let her do anything stupid—like get married!'

'Is that what happened to you?' Giles took his chance. He needed to know.

She studied his leonine face, the glorious dark blond hair, the strong features and the little lines of tension and, perhaps, strain, under his eyes, furrowing his brow. How good it would be to talk to someone who knew what it was like. How much she wanted to unburden herself. But dare she with this man?

'Yes,' she said slowly. 'We married far too young —just kids fooling around. Then Dan came along and things got a bit too complicated. I couldn't be the sort of wife he'd wanted me to be and he wanted his freedom. It was as simple as that. And you?'

Her candid gaze, full of conflicting emotions —relief, slight distrust still, confusion—swept him as he quietly took it all in. He shrugged, but she saw what the casual attitude cost him. He was as deeply scarred as she was. Her heart went out to him and she waited silently.

'Classic medical marriage, I suppose. My wife thought it would be glamorous to marry a surgeon and live in relative luxury. But the more she wanted, the harder I had to work. She didn't like the lifestyle or the hours I kept. We stayed together for my daughter's sake, but about four years ago . . .'

The hubbub of the busy restaurant went on all

round them, yet seemed to leave them untouched,
as if they were a little island of calm and tension in a
sea of noisy jollity. There was a long moment of
communion, and Louise wanted to reach out and
touch the man opposite her, reassure him, help
him—but years of restraint had left their mark.

'I know. My husband found himself another
woman.' Her voice was as cool as she could make it.

'And my wife found herself another man.' They
managed a grim smile each. 'So, we're about even,
aren't we, Louise?'

'I suppose we are. Rejects, both of us. She held
up her glass in a sudden, mocking toast. 'But what
about your daughter? Did she go to live with your
. . . with your wife's new husband?'

'Yes, for a year or two. But they didn't get on, so
she asked to come to live with me. I'd had a hard
time, wasn't really ready to have a teenage girl
living with me. I'd been living in digs, didn't have
a house . . .' He sighed and closed his eyes momentarily as if to blink back unhappy memories.
'Everything I'd valued seemed lost, so I couldn't
see the point of doing all the usual things that were
expected of me. I threw up my job, went to Nepal
on a health project—but it didn't seem to ease the
hurt much. I came back, lived in a grotty flat, drank
too much . . . And then Becca came to see me one
day and asked if she could come and live with me
. . .' He stopped again, the generous line of his lips
compressed at remembered pain.

Instinctively, as she would with any patient on
her ward, Louise reached out and took his hand,
covering it with her own.

'It's all right,' she said simply. 'I know.' Who
cared what the other diners thought about this

strange, quiet couple in their midst? Who cared
whether or not it was madness to get involved with
Giles Levete? Because involved she was; involved
because she had shared with him black moments,
because she knew how aching was the knowledge of
a failed marriage, through no one's real fault.

His fingers squeezed hers. 'This is ridiculous! But
I do want you to know. Becca came back . . .'

He stopped as the name finally made an impact
on Louise and her eyebrows shot up. 'You've got a
daughter called Becca? A tall girl, stunning, very
sensible, long blonde hair?'

'Tall and blonde—I wouldn't call her sensible.
Why?'

'I know her. She's . . . !' Louise suddenly remembered what Giles had said about his daughter
going about in the company of young louts . . .
'she's a friend of my son. I've met her,' she finished
lamely. 'She's a lovely girl.'

'A lovely girl I'm sure, but I hardly see her. She's
left with most of the housework to do because I
can't cope with it all, and she's out most of the time
gallivanting with her friends. I'm not much use as a
father, Louise,' he sighed despairingly. 'She came
and asked if we could set up home together, she
pulled me out of my depression, and now things are
falling apart again. How did *you* hold your life and
your work together?'

Louise blushed and removed her hand from his
grasp. The feel of his tensed fingers between hers
had begun to affect her in a complex way, one
which she was not used to. She'd coped by becoming icy Sister Slater, hadn't she? By working twice
as hard as anyone else, by trying to be the perfect
sister, the perfect mother.

'Ah!' He guessed the answer to his own question. 'Enter super-Sister! Was that it? If you were tough enough and distant enough, no one would dare question you about your private life.'

'It worked, too,' Louise smiled wryly as the waitress took their cold, half-eaten meal away. 'It did until recently, anyway.'

'So I've got to turn to ice, have I? No taking attractive women out to dinner? Not thinking of myself or my own happiness, but putting everything I've got into my daughter and my work? Do you recommend it, Louise?' His eyes were shrewd, piercing, seeing right through her to the turmoil he'd started within her the moment their hands had touched, relighting something long-forgotten.

Louise shook her head slowly, unable to meet his gaze. 'No,' she murmured quietly. Then more firmly, 'No!' And then her face was buried in her hands and the choking tears began to rise. Suddenly Giles's arm was round her as he left his own chair and came to her side. She struggled to hold back the tidal wave of pain that threatened to grip her, heard murmured voices above her head . . . And then Giles was saying calmly, 'I've got your coat and we're going to be allowed to slip out the back way, through the staff cloakroom. Come on, Louise.'

His arm went round her again and he helped her to her feet. Briefly she was able to shrug on her coat, give an attempt at a composed smile to the people sitting at the next table, and then they were slipping through the shabby back corridor of the wine bar, out past the toilets and into a back alley, from there to the darkened street . . . and before Louise was quite aware of what was happening, she found herself sitting in Giles's Rover.

She seemed to cry for ever, quite oblivious to his presence, to his arms cradling her, his fingers gently soothing her brow, his whispered words of comfort, but it was really only twenty minutes until the storm passed.

'I'm so sorry—what a fool I've made of myself,' she sobbed with embarrassment, ashamed to look at him, withdrawing to her side of the car. 'What must you think? I *never* cry—I don't know what's wrong with me . . .'

'Perhaps that's the problem,' he suggested, handing her some more tissues from the pack in the glove compartment. 'It's the one big drawback to the sort of life you've been leading, isn't it? You can't present that cool, composed face for ever or you'd go quite mad.'

He leaned across and turned her tear-stained, swollen face to him, studying her features in the light of the street lamp, tracing a stray tear with his thumb. His eyes seemed darker, full of something that almost frightened her; not mockery, not contempt, but something more than that; something that couldn't be easily dismissed, shrugged off. Something that seemed to penetrate her soul and assured her that he understood, that he knew what she felt—complete sympathy.

'How it must have hurt,' he said simply. And then his mouth was on hers, gently against her lips, and his arms were around her, holding her, reassuring her. For a minute she responded with all the despair of a woman who needed a friend, comfort —one who had almost come to terms with the fact that there was to be no man in her life, that she would be for ever on her own. Her arms came up round his neck, and her lips opened on a voiceless cry of despair and hope, and were joined by his own. Her hands were in his hair, springy and clean, and her body yearned for the long-denied union with his lean, firm, masculine flesh in a moment of complete madness. They clung to each other, Giles as stunned by the overwhelming sensations he experienced as he cradled her slim body as Louise was. Never again, he had said; never again would he risk himself for a woman, would he lay himself down to be destroyed. But with Louise in his arms, knowing what she'd gone through, finding the woman underneath the ice-cool exterior . . .

She stiffened against him, then pushed him firmly away, all her years of self-denial and self-sufficiency coming to the fore, telling her what a fool she was making of herself. What had she done? She'd fallen into his arms as if she wanted nothing more than physical comfort; she had broken down over a quiet dinner in a public restaurant . . . Humiliation and despair swept over her, where desire and frustration had been only moments ago. Anger, too, that Giles had been the one to witness her weakness and take advantage of her. She wanted his friendship and support, she admitted to herself now.

'Leave me alone!' The cry tore from her. 'The whole evening has been a terrible mistake!' She fumbled for the door catch, but the central locking system prevented her flight.

'Louise—' Giles's hands and voice urged her to calm down, but she couldn't look at him; couldn't bear to see the triumph and contempt which she feared she'd see in his eyes.

'Let me out!' Her struggles were frantic now, her

only thought escape. Oh, how the hospital staff would love to hear of one of their number reducing Sister Slater to hysterical tears! How would she face them?

'No—not until you stop all this self-pitying nonsense,' he ground out harshly. 'Aren't ten years enough time to have suffered? Do you want to go on avoiding life for ever?'

'You don't understand,' was all she could sob, reaching into her pocket for her own handkerchief.

'Yes I do damn well understand!' His voice was bitter but he reached out tentatively and put a hand on her shoulder. 'But I can't believe that you're going to allow something that happened so long ago to ruin the rest of your life. You can't forget it, I know—but surely it's time to try something new—'

'No!' Louise, as sensitive as if her skin was afire from his touch, shrugged off his hand. 'Just forget it. I'm not ready for something like this . . . not yet.'

'Something like *what*?' We're two adults who have been out to dinner together, that's all! You seem determined to believe that I've set out to seduce you or upset you in some way . . .' He slapped the steering wheel with his open palm and Louise wondered whether it was in lieu of slapping her face. Perhaps she had over-reacted to the whole thing. But how could she explain her fears; what it was like to re-enter a world of relationships that she'd excluded herself from for so long?

'I'm sorry, I knew this was going to be a disaster,' she murmured, swallowing back more tears.

'It's hardly a disaster.' Giles turned to her again, his bright eyes blazing. 'It's human—and I've seen remarkably little human behaviour from you in the

time I've known you, Louise. How many times do I
have to tell you that I *do* understand? I want to get
to know you, and if finding out about how badly
your past has hurt you is part of it, that's fine . . .'

'It's not fine by me! I'm not ready to start allowing anyone to get to know me, not yet. If you
wouldn't mind driving me home, Mr Levete—'

'Christ!' Giles's hands seized her face and twisted
it towards him. 'Is that all you have to say? You're
crazy. I want to take you out again, Louise. I want
to prove to you that you can have a good time like
everyone else—that you don't have to go on playing the martyr for the rest of your life. Or do you
enjoy it?' His face, lean and taut in fury and desire,
hovered over hers threateningly. 'Is that it? You
rather enjoy being the untouchable ice-woman
everyone fears? Well you don't frighten me!'

His mouth came down hard on hers, crushing her
swollen lips in a kiss full of frustration and
punishing desire. For the first time Louise understood just how powerful he was—and felt her blood
heating again at the sheer pleasure of being in a
man's arms. Her head told her to fight, but her
body and her heart both revelled in the dominance
of Giles's embrace. For a woman who had spent so
many years fighting her own battles, coping alone,
the arms of a strong man were comfort in plenty.
The feel of his lips exploring hers, his fingers pulling
gently at her hair, was enough to send tongues of
fire coursing through her. She responded, for the
second time this eventful evening, with all the
undisciplined instinct of a passionate woman long-
denied what she most craves.

It was Giles who broke away first, his breathing
unsteady and the pulse in his neck pounding in

protest. It would be easy, he thought to himself, to betray her now; she had forgotten herself, and he could do what he liked with her. 'I'll take you home,' was all he said, starting the car and pulling away into the light traffic on Highstead Hill.

Louise felt too stunned to speak—even to think. Her mind seethed with conflicting impressions and sensations—shame, anger at herself and with him for what he had said. And yet, despite all that, she felt an inner calm, for he had proved to her that she could trust him. That perhaps, given the chance, he might be able to make her happy. And yet, an inner voice warned, why should he want to do that? Why should he want to get mixed up with a woman who had none of the urbane style and accomplishments he'd want in his partner? What could she offer him? Advice, help with his daughter, she supposed. She could look after them . . . Was *that* what he wanted? A housekeeper, someone to cook and clean and generally make his life easier? Her heart sank. Someone who'd already proved herself capable by bringing up a son and could now do the same with Becca . . . With Becca? Louise ran a hand over her brow. Becca was such a good girl —so lovely! And Giles was the awful father complained about by both Dan and his own daughter . . . It was all too deep for her, especially at the moment . . .

The car drew into the kerb outside the house. 'Thank you very much for a—' Louise couldn't bring herself to thank him for a lovely evening; it would be so hypocritical.

'Thanks for coming.' Giles gave a shrug and smiled in the dim light from the street lamps. Should he ask her to see him again? In her present state he didn't want to create any more scenes. If she melted in his arms once more, offered her generous mouth to him again, he wouldn't be able to hold himself back, he knew. Oh, why couldn't things be simple, as they might have been with someone like Rosie? Why did this woman, complex and enigmatic, have to capture his imagination so thoroughly?

Louise waited a moment, hoping, despite all her newly born doubts and fears, that Giles would offer her another chance. But he seemed to have tired of her, for all he did was open the door and release her seatbelt.

'Good night, Louise.' His voice was thick— probably with anger at her ridiculous behaviour, she thought with renewed embarrassment.

'Good night.' She got out as elegantly as she could and made her way up the garden path. Giles, the door of the car still open, resisted the urge to call out after her, to beg her to agree to just one more meeting outside work—but, certain that he would be repulsed again, he bit back the impulsive words. What was the use? She would only mis-understand him; he could never hope to make her happy, only to add to her problems. A rush of protectiveness so fierce that it almost took his breath away caught him unawares; a sensation he hadn't felt for so long now he'd believed himself to be impervious to it. But protection was one of the last things he could offer her; first there came desire—and despite the fact that she obviously felt its keen edge herself, Giles wondered if she could ever accept him. Had she been too badly hurt? Had she had too many years of solitude and ice for him to ever thaw her heart?

Louise held the front door ajar for a minute, almost expecting to hear his voice or the sound of his footsteps as he ran up the path behind her with insistence that she stop, a vow that whatever problems stood in their way, they could be overcome . . . But all she heard was the sound of a car pulling away into the road. And what more did she have any right to expect, she chided herself. What more, at her age and with her responsibilities, and Giles with his own? Romance, love, hope for a future with a man she loved at her side—that was all futile now. She had had her chances ten years ago and tonight, her opportunities to live happily ever after, and she had blown them both.

Learn from it, Louise, she told herself, taking off her coat and studying her tear-streaked face in the mirror. It can never work. Once you loved Tony; once you felt just as you do now about Giles. And look where that got you!

But the cynical thought didn't help. Whether it had happened because they were right for each other, or whether because they both just happened to need each other at this moment she didn't know —but she was beginning to love Giles Levete. And there was nothing she could do about that.

CHAPTER SEVEN

WITH a practised eye Louise measured Mrs Hopkins' exposed buttock, found the right quarter for the injection, stabbed the needle home and followed the whole process up with a smart slap to diffuse any pain. 'Thank you!' she said cheerfully. 'That wasn't too bad, was it?'

'Not really,' muttered the patient, pulling down her nightdress and rolling over on to her back again. 'I wouldn't like to have it done too often, though.'

'You won't need to. This is just a shot of antibiotic to clear up the infection before it can get any further. It's always best to put it as close to the site as possible,' Louise explained for the second time. She dropped the syringe into the receiver, settled Mrs Hopkins in bed comfortably, and drew back the curtains. Normally this sort of job would have been delegated to one of the junior staff, but Rosie was unwell today, something to do with her sinuses —and to tell the truth, Louise actually rather enjoyed the mundane routine of injections and medicine rounds. She'd given a bed bath this morning, the first for months, and it had put her in a good mood; better than she had been in for the last couple of days, anyway. For since her scene with Giles Levete the other night, nothing had seemed to go right. Louise ran a hand across her tired eyes. The wretched man was even interrupting her sleep!

'Sister, do you have a few minutes to spare?' Mr

Amery, genial as usual, caught her as she trundled the trolley up to the treatment room.

'Of course. Who is it you've come to see, sir?' she asked, inwardly a little irritated that today of all days he should choose to pop down.

'Mrs Aitken—I can see from the look on your face that the problem hasn't resolved itself. I've asked Janet Bewlay to come along too. We must get this sorted out quickly.'

Janet Bewlay was the stoma nurse, and even her legendary patience had been tried by Mrs Aitken's stoical insistence that she would not help herself. The situation had deteriorated quite rapidly in the last few days, with a pressure sore and other problems developing—all of them due to the patient's determination to hinder her recovery as much as possible. The psychiatric counsellor had come down to try to talk over general matters; a social worker had been brought in to advise on the Aitken's home situation—it wasn't unusual for some patients to become 'addicted' to hospital life and then try to stay there. But nothing had done any good. Mrs Aitken still refused to take any responsibility for her care, to wash herself or to manage the colostomy bag. Her husband rarely came to visit and had evaded attempts to talk to him. It was most disturbing.

'We certainly must,' Louise agreed, spotting Janet Bewlay's ginger curls as she came through the ward doors. 'Would you like to talk over the case in my room, Mr Amery, or shall we go straight to the patient?'

'Let's go and see her now,' he decided after a quick flick through the notes he carried. 'About the only suggestion I can make at the moment is that we

"bribe" her with an offer of a week or two's convalescence if she'll co-operate with us now. Apart
from that, I'll give her a stiff talking to. But I'm
afraid the remedy remains in your hands, Sister.'

'I thought it might,' Louise smiled wryly as the
little group set off up the ward. Mrs Aitken saw
them coming and covered her face with the bed-
clothes, vainly attempting to pretend that she was
asleep as they approached.

'Now, Mrs Aitken,' the surgeon started firmly,
once the bed curtains had been drawn, 'will you sit
up properly? We want to talk to you and try to work
out what we can do for the best—and we can't do
that, can we, with you hiding from us.'

Louise gently eased back the sheet and blanket
and a pink-faced patient shuffled up the bed.

'You've been having some trouble, I hear. Why
won't you co-operate with the nurses, my dear?
They're doing their best to get you back on your
feet again, but if you won't listen to what they have
to tell you and learn to help yourself, you'll find
yourself in all sorts of trouble.'

The trio waited expectantly, but Mrs Aitken kept
mum—a trick that had sorely tried the patience of
many a nurse on the ward.

'Is it that you haven't understood everything
we've been trying to show you?' Janet tried, knowing full well that she'd explained what Mrs Aitken
needed to do until her face was blue.

'Perhaps there's some problem at home that's
worrying you?' Louise added.

'Lot of nosy-parkers, all of you!' the woman
exclaimed. 'I didn't want this operation, you all
know that, but you insisted I had it and so now
you've got to live with it.'

'You're wrong there, I'm afraid,' Mr Amery said flatly, seating himself on the side of the bed and realising that, for once, he hadn't received a glower from Sister Slater for doing so. 'As I explained to you when we first met, this operation was all I could offer you. You understood the facts and the problems and accepted them. You signed the consent form for the operation too, didn't you? But now you're behaving in this silly fashion, occupying a bed we'll need for other people with serious illnesses and wasting the time of Sister and Nurse . . .'

Janet raised an eyebrow at Louise over the surgeon's head. Neither of them had heard Mr Amery in quite this mood before. They both knew that they could never speak to a patient in this way and it was refreshing to find that he took their version of the story for the truth and acted on it. So many doctors left their nurses feeling frustrated by always siding with problem patients and refusing to believe that their behaviour was as bad as it really was. There was only so much a nurse could take, even if she was supposed to be the modern equivalent of a saint!

'I don't feel well,' was all Mrs Aitken would say. When pressed, she agreed that it might be because she refused to do what she was told—like getting out of bed and taking some light exercise. Mr Amery quizzed her further. Why didn't her husband want to talk to the staff? Were things all right at home? Stubbornly she insisted that they were.

'In that case you'll want to hurry up and get back there,' he observed briskly. 'So why aren't you doing your best to recover?' There was another strained silence. 'I was,' Mr Amery added tightly, 'going to recommend that you went for a few days' convalescence—but I really don't think you'll be well enough to go.'

Mrs Aitken's interest was caught. 'Where would that be?' she asked quickly.

'Somewhere down on the south coast, near Hove, I expect.' The surgeon's brow rose in a mischievous arc. 'Why? Would you like a few days away from Highstead, Mrs Aitken?'

'Of course I would,' she said crossly. 'And I've a sister who lives in Brighton, so it would be nice to see her for once in a while.'

'I'm afraid that you'd have to be able to manage your condition before you went—and according to Sister and Nurse Bewlay here, you've so far been unwilling to learn. How long would it take, do you suppose, for you to . . .'

His words were cut short by a shriek, and Louise excused herself immediately, running out to see what had happened. In the entrance to the toilets, in a small block off one side of the ward, she found Jenny Rees bending over a patient who should not have been ambulant.

'What's happened here?' This kind of accident was one which could be easily avoided by vigilance —Louise didn't like the idea of any of her patients slipping and injuring themselves.

'It's Miss Ransom,' Jenny explained. 'She was out of bed, as instructed. Apparently she took it into her head to go to the toilet on her own—I *did* tell her not to, Sister.'

Together they helped the woman to her feet —but already there was a trace of blood beginning to show through the dressing under her thin nightie, which they checked when they finally got her back into her bed, and Louise immediately called a doctor down to see her. 'I think it's only stitches that you've pulled,' she told the anxious woman. 'But we'll have to have someone take a look at you, all the same.' It was a good job that Mr Amery was on the ward after all, Louise thought. What a day for awkward patients! Every so often you came across one or two who seemed to think that the hospital was some kind of hotel and who were certain that they knew what was best—but just lately there had been a whole spate of them, and it made life difficult for everyone.

Mr Amery was able to confirm that no serious damage had been done and to write up a pain-killer for Miss Ransom and Louise was kept busy for the next few minutes, re-dressing the wound, staunching the slight haemorrhage with a pad of adrenalin, and replacing sofra tulle and gauze over the site. Miss Ransom was apologetic, which made the whole thing easier, and promised not to do anything so rash again.

'We have ways of making sure you don't!' Louise wagged her finger cheerfully. 'Honestly, Miss Ransom, we *do* know what we're doing. You just concentrate on getting better while we do the decision-making for you. Right now, though you feel quite strong, you're not ready to go for a walk.'

'I realise that now,' the woman said. 'But I felt so well!'

'Good—that shows that we're looking after you properly. You'll soon make a good recovery, so long as you take it easy.'

'I'll try,' Miss Ransom smiled. 'I'm just not used to being waited on hand and foot!'

'You'll soon get used to it, I assure you,' Louise

assured her with amusement. 'The problem comes when you go home again!'

In her office Mr Amery was waiting for her to return. 'All systems go, as usual, I see,' he commented sympathetically, 'so I won't keep you more than a few minutes, Sister.' Louise motioned to him to sit down, sinking into her own chair at the desk. 'I've managed to persuade Mrs Aitken to look after herself—'

'I thought bribed was the operative word,' Louise laughed. 'Whatever it was, I'm glad that it worked! When do you think we'll be waving her off?'

'Probably about the beginning of next week,' the surgeon said. 'From what Nurse Bewlay and I finally managed to get out of her, she's simply been depressed. Apparently her husband hasn't been able to transfer off night shift and so hasn't been in much to see her. That and the normal trauma of the operation . . .' He paused. 'I know you're not keen on tranquillisers, Sister, but would you object if I prescribed a short course of Valium?'

'It's not really my place to object,' Louise began carefully. 'But will it really help? We can monitor her in here and try to bring her out of it without recourse to drugs, surely?' She frowned—she was putting it badly and could tell from Mr Amery's expression that he didn't like what he was hearing. 'I simply don't like the idea of starting her on drugs she may not need. It's quite natural to be depressed by something like this,' she pointed out reasonably.

'Very well, Sister, I'll respect your wishes. But if Mrs Aitken seems to you to be getting more depressed rather than pulling out of it, I'd like to try anti-depressants.' He got up to leave and Louise accompanied him to the ward doors feeling a little annoyed that she'd had to present such a negative view. But too many women started on a 'short course' of drugs that lasted for years and made them dependent. Mrs Aitken would very likely get over the problems of her colostomy without too much trouble; there were too many doctors who saw tranquillisers as a universal cure.

Carolyn was just coming back to the ward with her arms full of X-ray folders as Mr Amery emerged, a rueful smile on his face. 'Thank goodness,' he murmured as he held the swing door for her. 'I'd heard a dreadful rumour that Sister was beginning to go soft—I even sat on the bed this morning and she said nothing about it. But I've just had a timely lecture on the evils of anti-depressants, so there's no need to worry!'

Carolyn grinned. 'Just an evil story put out by her detractors, I expect. Sister's like the ravens at the Tower of London. They say that when the ravens leave, the realm will crumble, don't they? Well I reckon that if Sister began to soften up, Highstead would fall apart!'

With a chuckle of agreement, Mr Amery disappeared up the corridor.

Louise sat at her desk, trying to collate information requested by the administration department for one of their surveys, but her concentration kept lapsing. Thoughts kept flickering through her head, even as she consulted the ward records and added up numbers on her calculator. Not just thoughts of Giles Levete, though his face was prominent in her mind—as were the memories of his kiss, the way he had held her that night in the car, and his apparent indifference since then. She had seen him only once, fleetingly, when he appeared with his young registrar to see a patient due for Theatre. Since the patient had gone to ICU and wouldn't be back on Women's Surgical for a couple of days, she didn't have any opportunity of seeing, or talking to him. Not that she *wanted* to see him, she chided herself. For after all, how could she face the embarrassment of actually having to talk to him again?

But it was no use pretending. No matter how painful it might be, she did want to see him, talk to him . . . perhaps even lie in his arms for a while, safe from all the pressures of this mad world. Other things had happned to worry her, too. She had come home the other evening to find Becca in Dan's room, both of them strangely bright eyed and nervous, and though Dan had grudgingly insisted that nothing had happened and that they wouldn't do it again, Louise wasn't sure how much she could really rely on him. The first flushes of youthful passion were difficult to resist, particularly with their parents conveniently out of the way for hours at a time. She wanted to trust Dan but knew, in her heart, that she couldn't. All she could do was hope that Becca was sensible. Anyway, perhaps she was making a mountain out of a molehill. They had to start finding out about sex at some time, didn't they?

She sighed over her paperwork. If only it wasn't so confusing! Was that why Giles had suddenly begun to figure in her thoughts—because he could provide the back-up and support she felt she needed at this moment? It wasn't a very promising foundation if it was true. He needed a house-keeper; she needed a man around, someone to reassure her that things would be all right and that she was going about the job of being a mother properly. A fine basis for a relationship!

Something else had happened to worry her too. She'd been going through the pockets of some jackets which she had intended to take to the dry-cleaners when she'd found Dan's post office savings book. It had fallen open on the floor—and though she didn't like to pry and rather prided herself on the fact that she didn't insist on knowing where he was going or cleaning his room, she could hardly help but notice that he'd recently taken more than two hundred pounds out of the account. But what should she do? She doodled on the back of a spoiled blood test authorisation form, her mind in turmoil.

If she asked him what he'd done with the money he'd get furious. Perhaps he had opened a bank account somewhere? Perhaps he'd found something useful to do with it? But Louise couldn't quell her fears. He hadn't bought new clothes, she was certain of that. What on earth could he want more than two hundred pounds for? She would have to ask, she knew. And if there was a huge row, Dan flinging recriminations about her prying and the fact that he was old enough to do what he wanted with his life and his wages, she'd just have to weather it. Things had never been like this between them before, though, she thought gloomily. Not until Becca and Giles Levete had moved into their lives had there ever existed this kind of gulf in communication between them. Was this what growing up was all about? She sometimes saw Dan for only half an hour a day, what with the shifts she had to work and the fact that he and Becca spent most of their time rehearsing for the school play. It hurt, too, that now he had Becca he didn't seem to want to spend time with her, his mother. It was understandable, all right; in her head she appreciated all the reasons. But there was no accounting for the heart, with its need for stability and its fear of loss. Perhaps my interest in Giles is an attempt to compensate, she wondered. It was all too complicated. How could she divide up her feelings and be sure that what she felt for the sardonic Mr Levete had nothing to do with the fact that her son was growing up and didn't need her any more. Giles did though . . .

She bent her head to the statistics on the desk and tried to work out what they meant before completing the form and moving on to updating files. Then it was time for another medicine round, then lunch —and having dealt with the unexpected arrival of an emergency perforated ulcer and thus missed the first half hour of her Sisters' meeting, it was well on the way to four o'clock when Louise finally donned her heavy navy coat and gathered her things together to leave.

The reception area of the hospital was busy. Visitors were still coming and going and, unusually, there was a small outpatient clinic in progress. There were also a fair number of people in plaster, waiting to be sent home by ambulance. At this time of year, with pavements slippery with wet leaves and the first frosts silvering the ground, there were always a fair number of fractures, particularly among the elderly. Though Highstead didn't have an official casualty department, it wasn't policy to turn away those people who had come to view the place rather as their local GP surgery. There was usually someone in the plaster room who could cope with an extra case.

Louise hurried through the warm, antiseptic atmosphere, turning up her coat collar as she went. It was chilly outside; the hospital was kept warm, and sometimes the shock was more than bracing. At the very moment that she arrived at the main doors an ambulance drew up at the bottom of the shallow steps—and she saw with consternation that the crew intended to bring a stretcher in through General Reception.

'You can't bring a case in through here!' She was down the steps in a moment. 'There's no Casualty Department here,' she told the bemused ambulancemen, who were wondering who she was until they spotted the neckline of her uniform peeping out from under the coat.

'We were supposed to take him to St Margaret's,' one of them said rather huffily, 'but they couldn't take him—they've got a major RTA. You're the nearest.'

'What is it?' Louise peered at the inert body under the pale green blanket. She turned to see if anyone else in Reception had noticed what was going on—after all, it wasn't her responsibility to admit or refuse patients—but no one had.

'Young lad,' the older of the two men explained. 'He's been glue sniffing and he's unconscious. The police found him on the heath. Haven't you got anyone at all who'll have a look at him?'

'Problems, Sister?' Giles Levete, tall and disconcertingly smart in a dark trenchcoat, had approached them quietly.

'A casualty case diverted from St Margaret's,' Louise echoed the ambulanceman's words. 'How

they were ever allowed to bring him in here I don't
know! All the ambulance services should know
that we don't . . .'

'All right, Sister, we'll sort out the rights and
wrongs of the situation later.' Giles gave terse
instructions for the stretcher trolley to be taken
round to the Outpatients entrance.

Louise cringed inwardly. She'd done it again!
Nerves at seeing him so unexpectedly had set her
off on the wrong tack. Now he'd think she was just
being officious. Gritting her teeth, she followed the
group as they traversed the few yards to the sec-
luded Outpatients entrance and went back into the
warm building.

Giles had already removed his coat and was
supervising the unloading of the patient into an
examination bay. He looked up as Louise entered,
surprised to see her still with them.

'Weren't you on your way out, Sister?' he asked
coolly as she joined him at the couch, taking off her
own coat as she came. 'You seemed anxious to get
away.'

'I wasn't anxious to get away at all—I just didn't
want to admit a patient if I didn't know we could
help him,' she replied, ignoring his barbed tone.
'Do you need a hand or not?'

A broad smile split the face that had so far shown
nothing but vague disapproval, and she saw his eyes
gleaming with accustomed amusement. 'Of course
your help would be welcomed, Louise. Can you get
him out of his sweater and arrange blood tests for
me?'

Already his stethoscope had been extracted from
the untidily crammed briefcase that had been
dumped on the floor. 'On second thoughts,' his

head came up abruptly, 'get the suction equipment and put out a call for a ventilator.'

It was obviously a worse case than it had at first appeared. Though it was years since she had worked in a casualty department, Louise leaped into action, finding the suction apparatus and wheeling it into position on the trolley. She proceeded to clear out the boy's throat while Giles ran tests for reflexes and carried out a perfunctory examination. As soon as she had done what was immediately required, Louise phoned through to Reception, and just a few moments later another nurse and a doctor were also standing around the bed.

'He's just very lucky he's here,' Giles commented as the two nurses cut the youth out of his messy clothing. It was obvious that he'd been sleeping rough for some time; his trousers were caked in mud, as well as the vomit that he'd almost choked on. As she worked, Louise felt her revulsion rise. The lad couldn't even have been as old as Dan, a voice inside her kept saying as she exposed his thin, pale limbs, badly bruised in places. He was such a pathetic sight that she could hardly keep the tears from her eyes. She took blood samples, then went off to inform the police that their case had been admitted here and not St Margaret's, as planned. By the time she got back to the cubicle, the boy had come round a little; the ventilator, unused, was wheeled away.

Giles was holding out the boy's arms, examining them for signs of injections, for although he reeked of glue it was impossible to know quite what he'd passed out on. 'Nothing here—thank goodness.' He looked up and found Louise's blue eyes misted

with tears. Gently he placed the battered limbs at
the kid's sides and walked over to where she stood.
The doctor and the nurse were deep in muttered
conversation and hardly noticed him leave the
bedside.

'What's wrong, Louise?' His hand on her shoulder was heavy and there was an impressive gravity
about him that made her want to walk into his arms
and stay there for ever. He was so strong, so
reassuring . . . But she couldn't do that. She
couldn't let him know what he had begun to mean
to her. Her pride was too strong for that. Would *he*
be able to swallow *his* pride and try again? Just how
brave was he? Because true courage was needed to
approach Sister Slater when she'd once slapped a
man down, she knew. Once or twice in her training
days men she'd refused had taken some pleasure in
telling her how cruel and destructive she was. It had
only made her all the more determined not to get
involved with another. Now, for the first time, she
was willing a man to approach her again and give
her one more chance to accept him.

'I'm just being silly—melodramatic,' she muttered, trying to smile. His attentive gaze sent blood
pounding to her cheeks and head. He was impossibly attractive; not in a film-star way, but a craggy,
dependable, experienced style. The fact that he
was there immediately made her feel secure, comfortable—even if he disturbed her pulse and his
image remained with her when he had gone.
'Seeing him there, he might be—'

'It could be Dan, you mean?' Giles's arm came
round her back, stroking her shoulder, soothing
her as he might do a frightened child. It was infi-
nitely reassuring. The boy on the examination

couch moved slightly, and both sets of eyes focused on him for a second. 'Your son wouldn't get himself involved in something like this, I'm sure,' he said simply. The timbre of his voice, so deep, so sure, made Louise feel like crying. How she wanted to hear him whisper endearments to her again in that broken, husky tone. How she wanted to know that *she* was wanted. At last, here in this pathetic little cubicle, with a glue-sniffer for company, the true nature of what she felt for this blue-eyed surgeon was becoming apparent to her for the first time.

'Plenty of well brought up kids go off the rails. But what can the parents be doing to let it happen?' she asked. And suddenly her mind conjured up visions of that two hundred pounds, suddenly gone missing from Dan's savings. How could *any* parent be sure what their offspring were up to? Even the most vigilant, the most determinedly understanding, could be caught out.

'What's wrong?' Giles sensed her worry. He pulled her through the curtains and into the next cubicle, empty and newly-scrubbed after the day's Outpatient clinic. 'Why are you suddenly worried about Dan? From what I heard, he's every mother's dream!' His hands claimed her own, and Louise felt the pressure of his thumbs as he ran them over her palms in a strangely intimate caress that took so much for granted. A month ago she would have pulled away, perhaps slapped his face; certainly she would have said something designed to ensure he never tried it again. But none of that had worked with Giles. He had persevered—and without knowing he'd done it, he'd won her heart.

'It's nothing . . . It just made me realise how

little time I seem to have for him. If he got into trouble, would I know about it?' Her brow furrowed and she leaned into the warmth of his body, all trace of the old Sister Slater, who'd have been shocked at such goings-on behind curtains, banished.

'I know. I get home and find myself wondering where Becca is and what she's doing. She could live a secret life and I wouldn't know about it.' He attempted a smile, but it didn't quite work. 'We can't live our children's lives for them—you've made that plain to me, Louise. And,' he did chuckle now, 'if it's any reassurance at all, statistics show that kids from one-parent families aren't really any more likely to get into trouble than others!'

'I do trust him. And in his way he's very loyal to me—still comes on family holidays, still helps in the house. But he has his own life now; he becomes more like a stranger every week.' Louise focused her eyes on the buttons of Giles's shirt, aware of the fresh smell of soap and tweed surrounding him. This was crazy! It would only take an inquisitive nurse racing past to flick back the curtain and the world would know her final secret. But she couldn't draw away.

'I'm not going to kiss you here.' Giles's lips were only a fraction of an inch from her ear, his voice low and with the faint unevenness that told her that he was feeling the tension between them too. 'You'd only slap my face if I tried to now, wouldn't you, Louise?'

She said nothing, but allowed her index finger to trace his throat, gently moving over the Adam's apple and up to his ear and that wonderful honey-

coloured hair, so naturally exuberant. If he were to
kiss her now she'd let him; she'd respond in the only
way any woman knows to tell a man how much he
means to her—how much he is wanted.

'I did warn you!' His mouth brushed hers, ex-
perimentally at first, for he was still unsure of the
reaction he'd receive. She was such an unpredictable woman, was Sister Slater. One moment so
officious, ready to turn away a patient delivered to
the hospital by accident and the next almost in tears
because of the lad's feeble condition. He wanted to
hold her, mould her, teach her to be soft under his
hands, to express all the warmth and concern that
lay hidden under the image she had purposely
constructed for herself and which he alone seemed
to have discovered. He wanted to make her laugh;
to see tears of joy and ecstasy on her cheeks, not
these constant frowns of worry and strain. Damn
it—he didn't want to see the woman he loved
forced to be tough and strong alone in the world,
against all odds . . .

His mouth came down harder, and he felt her
respond in the way she had before, the way he had
lain awake at night reliving, torturing himself with
regret for not following her into her home, banging
on the door until she was forced to let him in. And
then, in his imagination, he'd pulled her into his
arms, told her he loved her, seen her melt, just as
she was doing now, sighing his name in his ear . . .
Could they ever hope to be together? With two
careers, two children? His kiss faltered and he
found Louise's sea-deep eyes on him, aware that his
mind was only half on her. At that moment the
noise of feet and voices speaking at normal volume
interrupted whatever might have been said.

'Must be the police. I'll go and have a word with them.' Smoothing his hair with one hand, Giles backed out from the cubicle and soon Louise heard him telling the policeman what had happened. Disappointment hammered in her head. Despite what he had said and done, she had been painfully aware that his thoughts had been elsewhere, even as he kissed her. She'd said his name on a broken breath, and he'd scarcely heard her. She had her answer now, anyway. He was attracted, sympathetic to her plight still—but his romantic thoughts were elsewhere. And how could she blame him?

Pulling aside the curtain, she slipped back into the cubicle. Only the nurse was there, registering the lad's blood pressure, and she smiled as she looked up.

'It's okay now, Sister. He's round, and although he's feeling dopey he'll be fine in a few hours.' As if to confirm her report, the boy groaned and tried to turn over. Louise's hand, restraining him, looked large and capable on his bony shoulder, though in fact it was small and compact.

'How did you get into such a state?' she asked, and there was a touch of compassion in her voice that sparked him.

'I've been having a good time,' he muttered almost incoherently, still high on the glue fumes.

'How about your parents? Does your family know that you've been sniffing solvents?' She kept her hand on his shoulder and bent over him, so that he didn't have to move his head to see her.

'They don't bloody know,' he managed, sputtering, 'and they're not likely to care, neither.'

'Do you want to give me your name and address so that I can get in touch with them, anyway?

Anything you say to me is in confidence, I promise,' she added.

'You're joking!' He gave a snorting sort of laugh and twisted away from her touch. The nurse gave her a sympathetic frown.

'The police are here anyway, and they'll want to talk to you about where you got the solvents from. You'll have to give your name and address to them,' Louise pointed out. There was no law against glue-sniffing as yet, so the lad couldn't get into trouble, unless it was for obstructing the footpath or causing criminal damage or something. 'I just thought it might be better for your family if they were notified by the hospital that you've been admitted, rather than contacted by the police.' The boy simply ignored her. 'Fine!'

His attitude infuriated her—yet who knew what was behind it? Life was complicated these days for adolescents. There were pressures on them unknown to her generation in the swinging sixties, a time of booming wealth and hopes, optimism and confidence. Was Dan resorting to escape like this boy?

With nothing useful to be done, for once she'd called Men's Medical and found him a bed there, the youth was quickly transferred, Louise put on her coat and walked out of the building. Giles was nowhere to be seen. He'd gone up to Men's Med with the policeman, to cause trouble up there, Louise thought dryly, by insisting on holding an official interview in the treatment room. It had been what had happened with the Higgins girl, not so long ago. Giles seemed to go in for these lame duck cases. Would he have as much sympathy for this lad as he had for pretty Miss Higgins? Louise doubted it, smiling wryly. He seemed to have a pretty poor opinion of boys in general—including Dan, if he numbered Dan among Becca's other male friends.

The thought rankled as she waited at the bus stop. Who in their right minds could call Dan a yob? It was obvious he wasn't! Perhaps he was sometimes a bit scruffy or flamboyant in his dress —she recalled his recent passion for baggy track-suits and running shoes, and his summer uniform of indecently short running shorts—but he was obviously not a yob. You only had to speak to him to realise how bright and lively he was . . . Or did other people see him differently? Would another person see him with eyes only for the bad, the unusual, the unorthodox? But he wasn't a punk, for goodness' sake, she reminded herself. And Rosie certainly hadn't thought he was a yob! It was obviously Giles being opinionated, or perhaps he hadn't even met Dan. That seemed unlikely, but he didn't seem to have put two and two together yet.

The bus was nowhere in sight when Giles's Rover pulled up at her side and the door opened.

'You dashed off very rapidly!' His voice was cheerfully accusing, his face split by the usual engaging grin. 'Let me give you a lift home, Louise.'

She knew she should say no, after that inconsequential kiss this afternoon, but the temptation simply to be with him for a few minutes longer was too much for Louise to resist. She climbed in beside him, settling her shopping on the floor and removing a can of spray oven cleaner from the seat. It reminded her sharply, even as she settled herself beside him, of what she'd suspected earlier—that his interest in her might be more domestic than loving. Would he even know what to do with oven cleaner? She doubted it. She couldn't see him kneeling on the floor with a Brillo pad and rubber gloves—accustomed as he was to rubber gloves in theatre! Was she supposed to take the hint and offer to clean his kitchen for him? She carefully opened the glove compartment, which proved to be full of assorted rubbish, and crammed the can in, having to force the flap to close.

'Sorry about the car,' he apologised nonchalantly. 'I don't seem to get time these days to clear it out. Never mind, it's all useful rubbish!'

'I'm sure it is,' she remarked, amused to observe that in so many ways the car was like him; excellent quality through and through, but left to run slightly to seed—like his good suits that all needed a trip to the dry cleaner, or his battered briefcase that had begun to go at the seams. Even, until recently, his hair, luxuriant, attractive, but allowed to get too long. Wellington boots cluttered the back seat, along with a plaid rug, bundled carelessly in a corner. A pair of binoculars in a smart case lay haphazardly at her feet, along with a plastic carrier containing salad ingredients. Her fingers itched to tidy up. Not because she was an interfering so and so, unable to abide mess, but she wanted to make his life easier, simpler, less chaotic. Never mind. As a father on his own, he'd soon learn that organisation was the key to fitting everything in!

'How about coming out for a drink this evening?' he asked unexpectedly as they turned into Louise's road.

'I can't. This evening I've got to be in for Dan,' she said regretfully before she'd had time to assess for herself whether it was the truth or an excuse.

'I've got a couple of things to sort out with him.'
Like the money problem, she thought grimly. It
didn't look as if it was going to be a cosy evening at
home; more like a major row.

'For God's sake, he's not a little kid! Surely he
can make his own dinner tonight!' Giles had pulled
into the kerb just outside Victor Inskip's house. It
had grown dark outside and as Louise turned in
amazement to look at him, all she could see were
pinpricks of light glittering in his eyes. There was
anger in him, despite all the understanding support
he'd offered so far. Anger that despite everything,
she was still trying to evade him. She'd not behaved
fairly, she knew; she had driven him too far.

'It's not that,' she placated, pulling gently at his
sleeve and undoing the seatbelt. 'I've got something to sort out with him tonight.'

His look was disbelieving. 'The classic excuse!
You know, Louise, Dan is more like a husband to
you than a son. As soon as things start happening
you wheel him out as your reason for not getting
more deeply involved.' He released his seatbelt too
and turned to capture her, pinning her arms against
the side of the upholstered seat. 'Don't keep on
playing games—kissing me at one moment and
offering feeble excuses the next! Give me one good
excuse why you won't come out for a meal with me
tonight.'

His eyes were glowing, whether with pure anger,
or with a mixture of frustration and desire, Louise
didn't know. His strength began to frighten her; no
longer comforting, she suddenly understood the
sheer maleness of him and the force of desire within
him. It was both terrifying and sensually exciting.
She shivered, but not with cold.

'I've told you, I have something to sort out with my son. Giles, we talked about it this afternoon. I don't see enough of him as it is!' It sounded shallow, even to her own ears.

'You won't give up one evening with him to see me? Is that it?' There was bitterness in his voice, and his hands tightened their grip on her arms. 'God, Louise, I've never pretended to understand you . . .' He sighed. 'That tells me what you think of me, I suppose. But it still isn't a good enough reason.'

'I don't owe you an explanation!' She struggled to free herself, but he seized her.

'No, not like that! Not again! You ran away once, but this time you're not going until I have a single good reason.' His body was close to her own, she could feel the heat of him in the silent car. Only the light of a street lamp, newly turned on and just glowing a strange blue colour, pierced the winter darkness. It scared her that he seemed to feel things so strongly, so quickly. She had wanted him, yes. But so fiercely, so passionately?

'I don't like you,' she spat out. 'That's a good enough reason, surely?'

'You liar.' His kiss was hard, punishing almost, and Louise tried to avoid his invading tongue, but he held her to him as if she was the most precious thing in the world and he would give his life rather than part with her. Gently he teased her neck with his teeth, nipping her when she tried to push him away, running the tip of his tongue over her hot skin, pulling the neck of her coat wide so that he could gain access to her ear, the nape of her neck . . . He pulled her hair out of its pins and she let him do it, unprotesting.

'Your hair's so beautiful,' he murmured, finger-
ing strands of it as they fell down around her face.
'Why do you make me so angry, Louise?' It was a
question that required no answer; he buried his
head against her again, and she ran her hands over
the smooth, lean muscles of his back, replying with
her exploring fingers and mouth until he groaned
aloud in her arms.

'I don't mean to make you angry,' she whispered
in his ear as he kissed her again and again in tiny
butterfly touches that made her heart contract in a
welter of sensual delight. 'It just seems to happen
whenever we meet.'

He dragged himself away from her pulsing skin,
and his eyes were dark with longing.

'You know, after the other night I vowed I'd
never ask you out again. I knew I wouldn't be able
to bear it—wouldn't be able to resist you. And
I thought you really didn't want me.' His voice
still held an element of questioning, of nervous
expectation.

'I do, but . . .' Louise faltered.

'There's always a damn *but* with you, isn't there?'
He drew back, smoothing his hair and shirt. 'What
must I do to overcome it?'

'I don't know.' Thoughts poured wildly in and
out of her head. She hated seeing him hurt and
confused like this, but what could she offer him?

'I do know,' she began slowly, pain evident in her
tone, 'that when you drove off the other night I
could have cursed myself for letting you go. I've
been waiting to tell you that I want . . .' The words
were so difficult to find!

'Want *what*, Louise?' He was back at her side,
bending over her, lifting her chin with one finger,

studying her face as if he wanted to make a painting of it from memory.

'I *do* want to—to go out with you . . . get to know you. But where do we start, Giles?' Louise couldn't help but smile ironically. 'We're too old for romance! It can't be like it was, all holding hands and planning a future . . . We've seen the future and we know it isn't always rosy. And besides that we've both got children to think of.'

'I don't know the best place to start either,' he growled, 'but this is as good as any. And don't go telling me I'm not romantic!'

His kiss this time was one of depth and passion, sweeping away all Louise's remaining doubts about that earlier lapse of attention in the Outpatients' cubicle. There was *something* here; what it was she couldn't yet be sure, but there was a magic between them, a bond, no matter how badly suited they might seem to the world. At her age it was quite ridiculous to fall for a man in this way, Louise knew. But suddenly she felt eighteen again, full of hope and love, as if the rest of her life were still an unknown wonder and the pain of the intervening years had never left its mark on her. She trusted Giles absolutely, and gave herself up to his kiss . . .

How long they sat together in the car she didn't know, but suddenly there was a terrific banging on the roof and the vehicle rocked and reverberated with the sound. They shot apart, Giles smoothing his shirt, Louise pulling her coat safely around her, and Giles pressed the switch that sent the window gliding smoothly down. Victor Inskip's bland face smiled in at them.

'Hello, you two! Fancy seeing you here, necking like a couple of teenagers!'

Louise saw Giles's hands ball into fists and tried to retain her own composure—not easy with the blood still racing through her veins.

'The kids have locked you out of the house, have they?' Victor laughed unpleasantly. There was something lewd about him, unwholesome, despite his forgettable features. 'How sad, eh! when lovers can't go home because of the children! A sign of the times, you might say,' he added with a wink.

'I've told you before, and I'll say it again, Mr Inskip—I don't believe in sharing my private life with my neighbours.' Louise's voice dripped with the ice only so recently taken from her life. 'Thank you for your interest, but it isn't appreciated.'

'Oh well—each to their own, I say.' With a withering look, he picked his way over the grass verge and approached his own house.

'Obnoxious little rat! If he wasn't such a pathetic specimen of humanity I'd break his nose,' Giles muttered. 'I hate the idea of you even living next door to him, Louise.'

'If you knew what he'd suggested at the party you might think up an even nastier fate for him,' she laughed. But inwardly her heart warmed at the sheer pleasure of hearing him speak so determinedly, so caringly, about her. 'Perhaps we'd better go in and prove him wrong. Would you like a cup of coffee?'

Suddenly she felt nervous at the thought of him entering her home; after all, it had been her cocoon for the past few years—her private world that few had been permitted to enter. Would he find it scruffy or laugh at the eclectic combination of furniture, carefully acquired over the years? It was too late to worry, though, for he was

already out of the car and holding open the door
for her.

'You wouldn't believe how long I've waited for
that offer,' he told her gently as he followed her up
the garden path.

CHAPTER EIGHT

'DAN MUST be home,' Louise whispered as she ushered Giles into the hallway. The lamp was on, and lit it in a cosy fashion. 'He's probably upstairs doing his homework, so there's no need to disturb him.'

Giles nodded casually, aware of her nervousness and feeling the tension himself. After all, the way Dan took to him might be a crucial factor in the development of his relationship with Louise. He liked the look of the place. It smelled good, too. Dan had obviously had supper, for the aroma of fresh cooking hung in the air. It was warm, comfortable, a little worn at the edges, but a proper home, not like his own newly-purchased house which he and Becca hadn't succeeded in making theirs yet.

'Come into the kitchen,' she said quietly, leading the way, and Giles found himself in a warmly decorated room, all pine and pot plants on the window sills. A movement around his ankles made him glance down.

'You even have a cat!' He picked Cosmo up confidently, and the old cat, who didn't automatically take to everyone who invaded his domain, purred like a locomotive and lay in his arms like a fluffy baby.

'You've made a friend there,' Louise smiled, bustling about, putting on the coffee machine. 'You can stay for dinner if you like,' she suggested, but Giles barely heard her, so busy was he with the cat, tickling his stomach and telling him how gorgeous he was.

'I'd love that,' he agreed with a dark gleam in his eyes as he looked up at her over Cosmo, who batted his paws ecstatically in the air. 'You've got a lovely house and a gorgeous cat. If you can cook too, Louise . . .' Whatever he might have been going to say hung in the air meaningfully.

'Why not have a look around? If you can bear to put *him* down for a moment!'

'I don't have to put him down, do I? He can come with me. What's his name, anyway?' Giles asked, spellbound by the revelation that what he'd sensed about Louise Slater had been right all along. She wasn't what she wanted the world to think her; she had a son, a home, a cat even, that anyone would be proud of. She was as warm and generous as he'd suspected at their first meeting. He could love a woman like this.

'Cosmo. Don't ask me why—my mother christened him that when she rescued him from his condemned cell. He was a bit of a wanderer in his youth, but he's getting old and settled now, aren't you, you old fleabag?' Her finger teasing the thick fluff of his stomach found Giles's, and their eyes locked above the tabby cat for a long, heart-stopping moment that had them both speechless. Finally, as she heard the coffee begin to drip through the filter, Louise dragged her attention back to reality, and not the glorious promise she found in his brilliant blue eyes.

'Go through to the sitting-room if you like,' she said with studied casualness. 'I'll bring your coffee through.'

'Okay.' With something like a sigh, he disappeared into the hall. Louise, hands shaking from an intensity of feeling she could hardly bear, set mugs out on the tray. If he was to become a close friend, a lover even, he would have to get used to the way she lived every day. No best tea service for Giles. He would take her as she was, she decided. Just as she was taking milk from the fridge, having set the oven to heat up the beef casserole Dan had helped himself to earlier, there came a shout from the sitting-room—and then a whole welter of voices.

'What's going on here?' Giles's voice was loud and angry, and as Louise dashed out of the kitchen and into the sitting-room, a nervous Cosmo skittered across her path.

'What are *you* doing here?' Dan's voice was just as loud, just as angry.

'Mum, what's happening?'

'This is Dan?' Giles turned to face Louise, and in the subdued lighting of the sitting-room she saw fury on his brow and lips.

'Yes—Dan, this is Mr Levete, Becca's father . . .' It sounded too bright, too false for the occasion.

'I know *that*,' Dan said moodily, and in the shadows behind her son Louise saw Becca sprawling on the sofa, apparently buttoning up her shirt. On the floor lay copies of Romeo and Juliet. Dan was flushed, his crew-necked sweater tucked accidentally into the front of his trousers.

'What's been going on?' Her question hung in the air unanswered. Giles looked accusingly at Dan, who stared at the Indian rug at his feet. It was Becca who finally broke the silence.

'*Nothing's* been going on, Mrs Slater. It's just Dad jumping to all sorts of silly conclusions. We were rehearsing one of the scenes from the play, that was all.'

'That was not all.' Giles's voice was a dry, angry whisper. 'You were so carried away, you didn't even hear us come in, did you?' Becca's gaze followed Dan's.

'We weren't doing anything you weren't doing outside in the car.' Dan's face was hard; in this mood he was like a stranger to Louise. Her horror was visible on her face. 'I went out to find Cosmo about half an hour ago . . .' he offered, and his eyes were bright with what Louise recognised, suddenly, as tears. Tears for whom? For himself at being caught halfway to paradise with his girlfriend? Or tears at finding his mother kissing a man in a car.

'Oh God!' Her hand flew to her forehead. 'Dan, I'm sorry.'

'You're sorry?' Giles sounded as if he was about to explode. 'Your son's in here making love to my daughter, and *you* tell *him* you're sorry? How about an apology for me, young man? Because you're not going to get the chance to get near her again, I assure you!'

'Dad! It wasn't like that! I love Dan!' Becca flew across the room to join Dan. 'You can't stop us seeing each other.'

'Oh yes I can.' Giles turned to Louise. 'I can't believe that this is your son. To think that all the time he's been one of the boys hanging around my home, worming his way into my daughter's affections! And now I walk into your sitting-room and find them half-naked on the sofa . . .'

'My son is not a yob.' Ice had crept into Louise's

voice and she took a pace back from Giles, suddenly seeing him in new colours. 'He and Becca behave perfectly when they're here. And,' she quelled his attempt to interrupt, 'although I agree with you that they should be more responsible about . . . showing their affections . . . I think it's very hypocritical of you to be so pompous!'

'Do you?' Giles's eyes were wild, and his hand beat time in the air as he spoke. 'You're lucky you have a son, Louise, because as the father of a daughter, I'll do all I have to to prevent her from falling into a trap that thousands of young girls suffer. I won't have her married and pregnant at eighteen!'

Louise blanched. Words had never made her feel sick before, but these did. He wasn't to know, of course, that he'd just poured scorn on the early years of her own life. He wasn't to know that he was reminding her of the gulf that lay between them. 'Don't be so ridiculous,' was all she could utter.

'I'm not being ridiculous. I'm just not going to let her ruin her whole life. Come here, Becca, we're going home.' Louise recoiled from the second unconscious blow. Had she ruined her life with just one act? It was something she had thought to herself in her blackest moments, but just recently she had seen hope for a new life offered. Now it lay ruined before her. This man was an ogre, without feeling. She could never forgive him now, never love him . . .

'I'm not coming with you.' Becca's tone was flat, adamant. 'Dan and I are engaged.'

She held out her left hand, and on the ring finger a small diamond blazed. Dan's arm came round her shoulders defiantly, holding her to him, and Louise saw something more than simple adolescent lust burning in her eyes. 'We're not playing silly games, Dad. We're serious.'

'I'd like your permission to marry Becca,' Dan stated clearly, and at her side Louise felt Giles's blood pressure rise to danger level. 'We *are* serious, Mr Levete. As soon as I finish school and can support us, we intend to get married.'

'Dan!' Louise's voice rang through the room. She couldn't conceal her dismay, though with a sudden rush of understanding—and relief—she realised where the money from his savings book must have gone. 'You don't know what you're saying! Please, I know that both of you are serious about this and don't want to be treated like children —but you simply haven't known each other for long enough to make a decision. You're far too young!'

Dan and Becca pouted rebelliously. 'We knew you'd say that,' was Becca's flat comment. 'But you can't stop us.'

'Oh yes we can. I'm glad for once to hear that you agree with me, Louise.' He turned with incredulity written on his face. 'As you've been providing them with house room and every comfort I'd begun to wonder if you'd been taken in by the romance of it all. I think you've been taking your Shakespeare a little too literally,' he said scathingly, kicking a copy of the play with his foot. 'The pair of you obviously think of yourselves as a latter day Romeo and Juliet.'

'And you two are just as bad as the Montagues and Capulets,' Becca shouted. 'I'm not coming home with you, Dad. I don't want to live with you. You've never got any time for me . . .'

Louise saw the pulse in Giles's cheek begin to quiver, then tick. His tall lean body was tight with tension. 'You *will* come home with me,' he said in a voice that threatened to break and reveal something more than mere anger. 'We're going home for a long talk, my girl.'

Becca stood her ground, clinging to Dan's arm, and Louise realised that despite the girl's veneer of confidence, and her innate good manners, she wasn't as mature or as sure of herself as it first appeared. By contrast, Dan looked calm and determined.

'And I want to talk to you.' Louise caught her son's eye. 'Becca, go with your father. We all need time to think things over and take back what's been said tonight. Neither of us,' she tried to drop the voice of authority, Sister Slater's voice, which she'd automatically adopted, 'is the monster we seem to be. You've both got to admit that when it comes to marriage we know more than you do.'

There was sullen silence. Then Becca took a step forward. 'Okay, I'll come with you,' she said grudgingly to Giles. 'But only because Mrs Slater says I have to.' She kissed Dan tenderly on one cheek and he stroked her hair and whispered a secret endearment.

'We'll go right now, before anyone changes their mind.' Giles brooked no argument. Reluctantly Becca joined him and the four of them moved into the hall. 'We'll get something sorted out,' he muttered thickly. 'I'll let you know what the arrangements are, Sister.'

The 'Sister' was not wasted on Louise. 'Thanks.' She allowed her tone some ambiguity, copying his old sardonic undertone, but inwardly her heart felt fit to break. Whatever they had had was gone, swept away in family wrangles. She had been right, only an hour ago, to point out to him that their lives were too complicated for a romance. Her point had been proved in the unhappiest way possible. Now he thought her irresponsible, a bad mother, stupidly encouraging the children in an adventure they weren't yet old enough to understand.

'You can have this back, Dan.' Catching Becca's wrist, Giles wrenched off the ring, despite his daughter's howl of protest and the aghast look on Louise's face. 'Here, take it. Becca won't be wanting it.'

'It's hers—I gave it to *her*,' Dan insisted, refusing to accept it. 'Let her keep it. What harm can a ring do?'

Louise felt a moment of pride in his honourable refusal. Giles, too, felt some grudging admiration for the lad. His intentions were good, even if they were also sorely misguided. He was more of a gentleman than his outward appearance indicated. For a second Giles wondered if perhaps he hadn't reacted over strongly to what he'd witnessed. After all, sex was a fact of life with attractive young girls these days, wasn't it. Becca was responsible, informed . . . If only the boy had had a male influence at home, he found himself thinking. *His* influence? If he hadn't walked into the sitting-room, would he have sooner or later found himself acting as a kind of father to Dan? Giles looked at Louise's pale face and felt a stab to his heart he'd long ago thought he'd armed himself against. But what could he do? Hadn't Louise herself said that their job as parents came first; their own lives came a sorry second. So be it. He offered the ring again to Dan. 'I don't want it,' came the stubborn reply.

'Well she'd not going to keep it—or any false hopes about something I'll never allow her to do.'

'I *won't* take it.'

Giles shrugged and, with a gesture he knew instantly to be silly and melodramatic, threw the ring back into the hall. It hit the picture rail, then the floor, and Louise watched it roll away under the table. Then, with Becca crying forlornly at his side, he opened the front door and led her out.

Mother and son watched each other for an age, stunned shock shadowing their faces. Dan was the first to break out of the trance.

'Why did you just let him take her?' he demanded hoarsely, already too manly to let the tears flow.

'Because I couldn't possibly have persuaded him to leave her here—and because I happen to agree with him on the matter of your engagement,' Louise replied.

'He's awful! He doesn't give a damn about her —he's never there when she goes home from school and the house gets in a dreadful mess . . . And though he lets her have her friends back, he's always nagging. I could look after her better than he does!'

'I dare say you could. But you don't also happen to be holding down a very responsible job at the hospital which requires you to be called out at all hours of the day and night. And you,' her voice rose, 'also have the advantage of a dedicated mother who cooks, cleans and generally ensures that your life runs smoothly. You probably

wouldn't be able to look after yourself for a fort-
night! As for this ridiculous idea of getting married
as soon as you've got a job—'

Dan's eyes were cold. 'What's he to you? What's
going on between you and Becca's father?' A sob
trembled in his throat and he rubbed a hand
frenziedly over his brow, as if to conceal a tear.
'I've got a right to know!'

'Oh, Dan!' The force of her scathing words made
Louise want to take them all back. There was
nothing like hitting someone below the belt when
they were already down. 'Why are *we* shouting
at each other? It's not us who's supposed to be
rowing!'

'Oh sure!' His voice was full of bitterness, a
bitterness that should have been unknown to him at
his age. 'You let him drag my girlfriend off into the
night and then you tell me that I couldn't take care
of myself! Come to think of it, you haven't been
around here much lately . . .'

Louise could scarcely believe her ears. 'You
know I have to work,' she said gravely, biting back
the anger that rankled inside. Who was it had said
that there was nothing worse than an ungrateful
child? Right now she would easily have agreed with
them. 'If I didn't work we couldn't live as we do.
And frankly,' she added, 'I need to work. I couldn't
bear to be cooped up all day in the house on my
own.'

'It just shows how much you care,' Dan muttered
quietly, aware that he was on shaky ground and
already knowing he'd gone too far. 'It would be
nice to have you home once in a while.'

Louise grabbed him by the scruff of his neck and,
though he was several inches taller than she, dragged

him into the sitting-room and plonked him into a chair. He didn't resist; indeed, something in him quite liked her forcefulness, the fact that she was giving him all her attention.

'How many times have we had breakfast together this week?' she asked matter of factly.

He thought. 'Twice.'

'How many times have we had supper?'

'Once,' he murmured.

'And why have we only had one evening meal together this week?' Her face was set. Oh, she loved him and longed to throw her arms round him and comfort him as she had done when he was a small child—but some lessons had to be learned this evening.

'I've been out to rehearsals twice. You were on a late once. And you were late tonight.'

'There was an emergency admission as I was leaving,' she told him firmly.

'Huh! Some emergency! Don't forget, I saw you kiss him.' Dan's face was intent upon hers, and in it Louise saw a plea for denial; for confirmation that he was the only man in her life.

'You're right,' she nodded. 'I did kiss him.' There was a pause. The sound of Cosmo scratching at the back door was all that could be heard in the house. 'Anyway,' Louise forced herself on, 'that has nothing to do with the fact that we haven't seen much of each other this week. We can spend the weekend together if it suits you, but you have your own life, remember. You didn't think twice about me when you had Becca to go out with. I've missed seeing you, but *I've* accepted that it's all part of you growing up. Now you're old enough to have a life of your own, you'll just have to start accepting that

I've got my own interests too.'

She could scarcely believe what she was saying. Where had the old Louise Slater, dedicated to her son, martyr to his happiness, gone? And she was speaking as if there was still some possibility of a relationship between her and Giles—and that, plainly, was quite out of the question.

'This has been very informative. Now I know just how much I'm wanted around.' Dan stared at his hands in a gesture Louise recognised from her own repertoire. 'I'm sorry I get in the way of your fun.'

'Don't be so stupid, Dan!' He tried to get to his feet, the tears trickling down his cheeks, his top lip bitten bravely as he tried to control himself. Louise put her arms round him, but he shrugged her free with little effort. 'I've given up my life for you, and until now I haven't regretted a single moment. But you're changing—you don't need me any more—'

'I thought I couldn't look after myself?' With typical teenage logic he caught her out.

'Not as well as I can look after you,' she waved the objection aside. 'I've never begrudged you a moment, Dan. I've felt so proud of you I could burst. But now I've found someone I want to get to know—someone I think I could be happy with when you've gone to make your own life. You found Becca and I found Giles. And now we've both got to accept that it's over . . .'

'All because of you and him. If you hadn't brought him here tonight it would all have been all right!'

'For you, you mean.' He heard her sigh, saw the pain in her eyes, the tears that had gone unnoticed in his own sorrow. 'I'm sorry I brought him home then,' she said simply. 'It disrupted your plans, so it's my fault, I suppose. All I hope is that you don't marry Becca or any other girl while you're too young to know what life's all about and then spend years regretting it.' She turned away from him and went out into the hall, crouching to retrieve the ring from under the console table. 'I really do hope you're not going to need that for a long time,' she told him, putting it firmly into his hand. Then, feeling as if she could barely move or breathe for the weight of despair welling inside her, Louise climbed the stairs and locked herself into her room.

Tears came easily. Tears of sorrow for the fact that now, at long last, she had managed to lose Giles without lifting a finger or her voice to do so. Tears of anger that he could behave so stupidly, so melodramatically. Tears of recrimination for herself, for tonight she'd shattered Dan's boyish dreams and expectations in a harsh, selfish way. She had behaved badly all round, she decided. She should have known much better than to get involved with Giles in the first place; that was her worst mistake. But she'd allowed herself to weaken, and then she'd compounded her weakness this afternoon by bringing him home. All those painful lessons learned so slowly over the years had been swept away in a space of hours. She was like a dieter who in one mammoth binge had undone months and months of strong-willed discipline. She'd been selfish and silly, imagining herself in love with him. At her age? Oh, it was laughable! And now she'd ruined her relationship with her son for ever . . .

She washed her face at the basin in her room, examining her skin and teeth as she did so. Faint laughter lines were already forming round her eyes.

She was beyond the first flush of youth. She was neat, attractive, but there was nothing here to entice a full-blooded man who could have any young nurse he wanted. Mature men, men with that extra dimension of ruggedness, as if they had been tested by life, tried by fire, and had emerged unscathed. Or perhaps Giles had been more deeply hurt than he cared to admit. Perhaps he had used this evening's opportunity to extricate himself from a situation that might have become too demanding.

Why did it have to hurt so? Louise wondered. Why couldn't she love lightly and leave lightly? How much easier everything would be then. She didn't really believe it, though. To love well and deeply was to risk the worst hurt. If one risked nothing then the prize was worthless. She should have learned her lesson a long time ago, but there was no fool like an old fool.

Strangely, when she thought about it now, she couldn't imagine what life would have been like if Tony hadn't left her all those years ago. It was impossible to think of them living in luxury, perhaps in America, perhaps with other children. Louise knew for a fact that his sort of life would never have suited her. She didn't like the superficiality of the art and design and TV circles he'd begun to move in before the break-up. Those sort of people seemed uncaring, concerned only with themselves—exactly the opposite to Giles' dedication and her own conviction that it was a worthwhile job to make the lives of others easier and happier, even if the job didn't offer a big salary and high status. Sometimes she missed having the support of a man around—but that man had never been Tony. He'd been faceless for years and years, though just recently he'd taken on the lean, harassed, blue-eyed features that made Giles so attractive. Somehow she'd always accepted that things weren't right with Tony, she realised now. She had loved him, yes, with all her heart. But even in the first months after her marriage the seeds of doubt were there. Perhaps, deep down, they'd both known that there was a flaw in the relationship. That their goals and ideals weren't exactly the same . . . Louise sighed. It was no good worrying about that now. Or about Giles. He'd gone. Now she'd lost both of them.

Footsteps came up the stairs, accompanied by the rattle of china. There was a tentative knock on the bedroom door. 'Can I come in, Mum?' Dan called gently.

Louise brushed her hair quickly and then went to open the door for him. He carried a big tray containing plates of scrambled egg and toast and a pot of tea, and he looked both embarrassed and hopeful.

'I thought you might want something to eat,' he offered tentatively.

'That would be nice,' she agreed, and he came in and set the tray on the dressing-table. Louise sat on the bed and he came to join her, pouring a cup of tea and handing her eggs and toast where she sat. It was the re-enactment of the picnics they'd had years ago when he was little and had wanted to cook for her. Because she worked shifts it was difficult for him to cook breakfast in bed like other kids, so sometimes he'd brought lunch or dinner, usually just baked beans, up into the bedroom and they'd shared the meal there.

'I remember the first time you made scrambled

eggs,' she smiled nostalgically. 'They tasted fine, but I never worked out what you did to ruin the pan so thoroughly. I had to throw it away!'

'I burned the first lot, so I made some more and then washed up before I brought you the eggs,' he replied, but the story didn't really interest him, she could tell. They ate in silence for a few moments, both uncomfortably running over what had been said earlier and what needed to be said now.

'I thought I might phone Mr Levete,' Dan started at last, carefully avoiding his mother's eye.

'I don't know if that's a good idea,' she said quietly. 'I really don't think he's in the mood for rational thinking at the moment, Dan. What were you going to say to him?'

'I thought I might promise not to talk to Becca about getting engaged or be alone with her.' Louise could see that his own tears had only recently stopped flowing.

'Leave it until tomorrow and I'll try to see him at work and tell him,' she promised. 'I don't think he's in the mood for promises now.'

'What do you think he'll do? He's so bossy . . .'

'I don't know what he *can* do, apart from having a good talk to her. He's only doing it because he cares about her, Dan. He's talked to me about her a lot—that's the way we first met, because he heard about you and wanted some advice on how to bring her up on his own.' She carefully edited out all the other meetings and confrontations that had been a prelude to their growing interest in each other. 'He's just as worried about the fact that he's not around enough as I am. And it's worse for him because he's so much newer to the game than I am.' There was more silence. Louise tried to control her curiosity but couldn't. 'What has Becca told you about her mum?'

Dan shrugged. 'Not much. They don't get on —or at least, she doesn't get on with the man her mum's married. He sounds a right nutter, worse than her father even. He wouldn't allow her out at night or anything, and her mother didn't try to make things easier.'

'But if things haven't been going well with Giles, why hasn't she gone back to her mother?' Louise's use of the Christian name didn't go unnoticed by Dan, but he said nothing.

'She felt sorry for her father, I suppose. After all, it was her mother who walked out on him after all those years . . .'

'He's not *that* old!' Louise laughed. Then, more seriously, 'Did you decide to stay here with me rather than go to your father because you felt sorry for me?'

'*No!*' Dan's eyes were incredulous. 'Honestly, Mum, when I went over to see him in New York he'd hardly got the time of day for me, and he kept sending me out sightseeing with all those women friends of his . . . They treated me like I was a little boy. One of them even bought me an ice-cream three times a day. It was obvious they were just using me as a way of getting in with Dad—and he knew it and was using them.'

Louise didn't know whether to laugh or cry at this unexpected news. 'I thought you'd had a terrific time over there! In fact I wasn't sure you'd be coming back to me . . .'

Dan's face fell. 'You didn't want me back?' he asked quietly.

'Dan—don't be stupid! Of course I wanted you

back! But your father seemed to have so much more to offer you than I ever could, and I'd decided that if you wanted to stay with him you could. For *your* good, not mine,' she finished. 'I don't know what I would have done without you—but you came back.'

He digested this information for a few moments, and she finished her meal. All this should have been said long ago, she knew. All these vague misgivings and doubts shouldn't have existed between them. Well, she had one thing to thank Giles Levete and this whole awful evening for, anyway—and that was the opportunity it had given her to clear the air with her son. The pain around her heart was a little relieved by that knowledge. If only it hadn't happened like this.

'I really do appreciate what you've done for me.' Her son's voice was muffled with embarrassment. 'Honestly, Mum, I know how hard it is for you on your own.' He stared down at his empty tea-cup. 'I'm sorry if I've mucked things up between you and Mr Levete.'

'There was nothing there to muck up,' she lied briskly. 'You're the most important man in my life, Dan, whatever happens. I want you to be happy, that's all. And I know from experience that getting married at your age is a terrible mistake most of the time. You don't have to take my word for it either. Just look at the divorce statistics. And every single one of them meant pain and heartbreak. I don't want to see it happen to you and Becca. You both need the chance to go to college, get out in the world and meet more people. If you're still in love after a few years, *then's* the time to make a commitment.'

'All right.' Dan's face was grave. Louise remembered how much she'd thought she loved Tony at his age and how they'd stubbornly refused to heed the advice of their parents. She knew what her son was going through. 'But I'll do it for you, not for her father,' he said flatly. 'And whatever happens, Mum, we'll have each other, won't we.'

It wasn't a question. It was said with such conviction that Louise felt her heart rise to her throat. 'Yes,' she assured him. 'Yes, whatever happens, you've got me—and I've got you.'

CHAPTER NINE

THE FACT that for the next two days Mr Levete made no appearance on the ward, choosing to send his eager young registrar, Steve Marsh, instead, was not wasted on either the nurses or the patients. Though it was not the only source of gossip—for Rosie Simpson, backbone of Women's Surgical and Sister Slater's sidekick for so long, had taken it into her head to resign.

Louise couldn't fathom out why; indeed, the news came as something of a shock, for whatever Rosie's drawbacks, no one could deny the fact that she was an excellent nurse.

'We're all going to miss you very much, Rosie,' she shrugged helplessly when her staff nurse came to announce the news. 'Are you going to move on to further training? Your Midder or health visiting? You'd be excellent at that.'

'No, Sister, I just wanted a change, and there seemed no point in hanging about,' Rosie responded vaguely, hanging her head in something like embarrassment. 'I've been here for so long now . . . I thought I ought to get some wider experience.'

It was plain that something had happened to induce her to make such a speedy decision, but Louise couldn't fathom out what that might be. 'Do you have something lined up?' she asked warmly.

'No. I thought I might take a month off and go to stay with my parents before I start looking for something new.' Rosie couldn't look Sister in the eye for fear that she would break down and cry. It made everything so much more difficult, Sister being so nice about this sudden departure when she had every right to complain that she should have been warned.

'Well, if you need a reference you know that you'll get a very good one from me!' Louise tried to lighten the situation with a little laugh, but it fell leadenly.

'Thanks, Sister.' Rosie almost stumbled across the room, her eyes misty with tears. Here she was, resigning because of Sister's relationship with Mr Levete—and Sister all innocent smiles and kindness about it. She began to regret her rash decision.

Perhaps I ought to do the same, Louise thought despondently as she saw her staff nurse go. Then she wouldn't have to see Giles and experience his anger and that stabbing pain of love that only he roused in her. But changing job wouldn't solve the problem of Becca and Dan, she knew. What they really needed was to sit down, all four of them, and talk it out. It was the only way. But from what she had heard, Giles was behaving far from reasonably. He had had his telephone number changed, so that when Dan called to apologise he got just an angry shriek. And Becca hadn't been at school either . . .

How stupid of Giles to imagine that he could lock his daughter away! That would lead to worse trouble, like running away. And yet Louise couldn't condemn him for what he had done. Her knowledge of him had shown her that he was a deeply caring man, and a man who had been very badly hurt by his past. She sighed deeply and rested her head on her hands. Things had looked so good.

Happiness had seemed within her grasp for the first time in years . . . Was it ridiculous to hope that everything could sort itself out? Oh yes, the hardened voice inside her insisted. It was sheer stupidity to hope for the unattainable.

A shy cough made her start with embarrassment at being caught deep in thought, and her cheeks reddened.

'Miss Callaghan!' Louise's voice was full of relief. 'It's nice to see you again. Come in and sit down.'

'I had to come to the hospital for Outpatients,' the elderly lady explained as she seated herself, 'so I thought I'd come across and tell you my news.'

'I can't wait to hear it,' Louise said brightly, thrusting thoughts of Giles to the back of her mind.

'I'm going to go and live in one of those sheltered places with a warden, in Buckingham. The sort of place you suggested while I was here. I know I wouldn't contemplate it at the time, but I was taken to see this place and it's lovely.' Her eyes gleamed with pleasure. 'So clean and easy to look after, and with a lovely view of the countryside . . .'

'It sounds ideal. I'm very pleased to hear it. And it's near enough for me to come over to see you once in a while on a Sunday,' Louise smiled. She paused a moment to bid whoever was knocking on her door enter. Giles's tall, lean figure moved briskly into the office.

Whatever there existed between them, whether it was love, as Louise thought, or maybe just intense sympathy between two unhappy people, had not abated in the two days since Giles's hurried departure from the house. The mere sight of him, so tall and strong, sent sensual memories coursing through Louise's veins. Giles swallowed the sudden constriction in his throat.

'This is Miss Callaghan, one of our success stories.' Miss Callaghan rose at his presence, as if she had suddenly found herself surrounded by royalty rather than an agitated consultant, but Giles had steeled his nerves for this encounter with Louise and hadn't bargained on the presence of a patient. He nodded brusquely to the old lady and then addressed Louise in a brisk, sharp fashion quite unfamiliar to her ears.

'I've come to sign the discharge form for Mrs Lofts, who's due out tomorrow. I won't be here —I'm going to inspect a school. A girl's boarding school.' Apparently for Miss Callaghan's benefit, but really for her own, Louise knew, he added, 'My daughter is getting a bit of a handful, so I think it's time she went off to school.'

'From my own experience, I'd say it's the children who are a handful who most need a stable home background,' Louise chipped in, irked by his tone and the way in which he refused to look directly at her. Suddenly the ice was back in her voice, her defences on the alert. Miss Callaghan, who was well-qualified to talk about schools and children, sensed that her opinion would not be welcomed and stayed quiet.

'*That* attitude explains an awful lot.' At last Giles's eyes met hers, and they were a glacial blue that glittered as he took in the gentle lines of her face and the tautness of her mouth. He forced his attention away and took the discharge form she offered. Forced almost to speak in riddles by Miss Callaghan's presence, Louise knew the frustration of being unable to say what she wanted.

'I think you're over-reacting, Mr Levete,' she murmured tensely. 'After all, you'd be very worried if Becca wasn't developing properly. Girls will be girls, you know.'

'And boys will be boys. Sister, and that's the trouble.' Giles bit the words out with an effort. He had willed himself to walk on to the ward and confront Louise in her office; he had vowed to himself that, come what may, he would nip whatever feelings there existed between them in the bud. But it was almost impossible with her here before him.

'That's a most unjust statement if ever I heard one!' Scorn dripped from Louise's words. 'Were you never a boy, Mr Levete? Or were you born with that sanctimonious head on your shoulders?'

'I think I'll just go and say hello to Nurse Simpson,' Miss Callaghan murmured as she walked stiffly out. 'She was always so kind to me.' But the surgeon and the Sister hardly heard her go.

'You know damn well that I'm capable of feeling everything a teenage boy feels, Louise, and a lot more besides. But I know when to call a halt.' His pen skidded across the green paper of the form, ruining it, and with a furious grunt he pulled another from the folder.

'I think you're using this as an excuse.' The words slipped from her lips before Louise had even formulated the thoughts, surprising her. 'I think that you wanted an excuse to keep you away from me, to stop you getting involved again, and that you're using Becca and Dan . . .'

'That's nonsense!' His lean head shot up from the desk, his cheekbones catching the light of the desklamp and seeming even sharper than ever. 'I don't want to have to do this, believe me, Louise, but I've come to agree with you. People in our position have to think of the children first. What we want doesn't count.' He was pale and the brightness of his eyes had begun to give way to something darker. 'I won't let Becca jeopardise her future for anything. Not even for you.'

'So you are prepared to hurt her by sending her away to school, *and* to hurt me?' Louise asked, her voice scarcely more than a whisper. Damn pride, damn all those years of reticence; she had to know.

'What choice do I have?' Giles ran his hand through his hair and wished he'd never plucked up the courage to come along. How could he bear to say these things to Louise? And yet he had to. 'There was something between us, yes, but it's got to end. How could we marry and have them living together in the same house? It would be impossible. And so we'll just have to finish whatever it was we started. So from now on, Sister, I hope we can have a businesslike relationship.' He stood up, so tall, so distant, and offered his hand, and even as she shook it she felt something, that old flame perhaps, ignite inside and begin to burn.

Giles could say no more. Mutely he hurried away, back to the surgeon's sitting-room. What had he done? His own pain he could bear, but the knowledge of the hurt he was causing Louise was almost impossible to live with. She was the only woman he'd felt this way about ever, and he had just thrown her away . . .

Steve Marsh looked up as Giles, ashen-faced and without a trace of his usual irreverent humour, returned.

'Job for you,' he said, handing Giles a notepad. 'We've just had a call from Farnley General. They've admitted a probable valve replacement and your friend Peter Prince there wants to know if you'll take him. He can't do it, apparently.'

'When can they get him over here?' Giles asked automatically, scarcely listening to the details. Yet if he was to forget everything that had happened in the past few weeks, work was his only answer. He would have no Becca to worry about in the weeks to come, no Louise . . . The fleeting thought of loneliness he brushed aside dismissively. But was he going to turn into the male equivalent of Sister Slater?

'A couple of hours—he's stable and no indication of an infarction from their tests,' Steve explained.

'OK, get him over here as soon as possible. We'll run tests on him this afternoon. Do we have any details?'

'Only a few brief ones.' Steve studied the notes he'd been given. 'He's an American, thirty-eight, over here with a film crew working at Elstree. He's a designer or something, no history of heart trouble. His name's Tony Slater.'

'Is it indeed?' Alarm bells rang wildly in his head. It had to be—it was too much just to be a coincidence. Louise's husband was back in town, and he was to be *his* patient.

Tony Slater lay relaxed and confident on the examination couch, the electrodes attached to his chest while Giles performed the angiogram with studious concentration. Another patient he might have talked to but the last thing he wanted was a conversation with this man.

'I'm going to inject some dye into the heart area and X-ray the results, just to check how your heart valves are functioning. You'll go along to X-Ray in a moment, and I'll be along in five minutes. Nurse will wheel you over there.'

'Fine.' Tony Slater listened and took it all in, smiling at the nurse as she removed the electrodes from his chest, which was a deep Californian bronze and liberally covered with hair. Giles wished he was more obviously objectionable, so that his dislike would be justified, but in fact he seemed perfectly pleasant. A bit too confident of himself, perhaps, but not unattractive.

'Listen, Doctor, I wonder if you could do me a favour.' Tony's voice held a Transatlantic twang, but his English origins were unmistakable. 'Is there a nurse still at this hospital called Louise Slater? I know she was here three years ago.'

Giles hesitated a moment, tempted to lie, but there was no point. Sooner or later someone would put two and two together and tell Louise that her ex-husband was in Men's Surgical. 'She's Sister Slater now,' he said flatly. 'She runs Women's Surgical. Would you like me to tell her you're here?'

'If you wouldn't mind—and if you don't think it will inconvenience her. Just tell her Tony's here. She'll know who you mean.'

'I bet she will,' Giles muttered under his breath. Aloud he shrugged, 'I've got to go over there anyway.'

'Thanks, Mr Levete. Wheel me away, Nurse!' With a quick smack of the young nurse's posterior, Tony disappeared to X-Ray.

'What do you make of these?' Steve Marsh, who'd been silently contemplating the angiogram readouts, held a length of paper out for Giles to see. 'Doesn't look very good to me.'

'Nor to me,' Giles agreed. 'Surgery is obviously on the cards. The day after tomorrow, if we can find theatre staff. Can you start making arrangements? I'm just going over to Women's Surgical to inform Sister Slater of her . . . of her friend's arrival.'

Giles's slip-up hadn't been lost on his registrar. Unlikely as it seemed, it looked very much, he decided, as if Mr Levete and Sister Slater had been caught out at something or other.

'Tony? Here? There must have been some mistake, Giles.' Or was he trying purposely to confuse her, to make his behaviour this morning more excusable? Louise's head reeled. It had been a tough morning on the ward; Rosie's news and her personal life were bad enough as things stood—but Tony . . .

'There's no mistake.' Giles could see the mistrust and conflict in her eyes and the spark of jealousy that had been nagging him since Tony Slater's arrival at the hospital began to grow within him. 'He's been doing some design work up at one of the film studios, so he tells me.'

'He didn't tell me! He didn't even tell his own son that he was coming over,' Louise fumed, her mind taken, for a few moments, off Giles's figure, so dominant and demanding, in front of her. 'If he hadn't been taken ill we would never have known he was over here. Oh, he's so irresponsible.'

Giles watched her reactions closely. He found it difficult to believe that Louise could ever have fallen in love with and married . . . it pained him to think of him by name . . . *that man*. Perhaps Slater hadn't been so cocksure and confident then. Perhaps he had changed. He felt an uncomfortable wish that he hadn't told Louise that her ex-husband was here. What if . . . Surely it was ridiculous to imagine that Louise would ever want to go back to him? And yet he couldn't be certain of that and the uncertainty hurt him.

'Well, I suppose I'd better go and visit him. Tell me, what is he in for? You said his heart, but he's only a youngish man. It's nothing serious, is it?'

Her concern hit him like a knife in the stomach; suddenly, with a blinding flash of realisation, Giles knew that he couldn't let her go—couldn't risk her falling out of his arms and into the arms of Tony. 'At the moment it looks like a valve replacement, though we won't know until later. So although it's obviously fairly major there's nothing to get frightened about,' he said, trying to comfort her as he would do the relative of any of his cases. Only this time it seemed difficult to be so reassuring, because his heart wasn't in it. His heart was with her. 'You can go and visit him on Men's Medical when you want. He's in X-Ray at the moment but he'll be with Sister Walsh . . .'

'Oh, I'm in no great hurry to see him,' Louise snapped. 'I'll come at visiting time, just like everyone else.'

'Right, Sister.' Giles's relief knew no bounds. 'Louise,' he added meaningfully, 'I'd like to talk to you later . . .' But Louise had turned back to the dangerous drugs cabinet and begun to tidy it as if her life depended on it, ignoring the warmth in his voice even though it kindled a glow in her heart and set her senses reeling. How could she trust him? No, it was better for the old Sister Slater to make her comeback. That way no one would get hurt . . .

'You look wonderful, Louise. Not a day older than when . . .' Tony came to an embarrassed pause, aware that whatever he said it would bring back unhappy memories. 'Nursing obviously suits you.'

'It does—but I think you need your eyes testing,' Louise said acerbically. 'Because I *am* fourteen years older than when I last saw you and it does show.'

Tony raised an eyebrow in worldweary surprise. Despite the way he had treated her, Louise had always been mild and compliant with him in the past. He had expected to find her the same, but he wasn't sure if he didn't like this self-assured version of her better than the old one.

One thing was for certain; *he'd* certainly changed, Louise thought to herself. He'd been on the fleshy side when she had married him and he'd had a full head of hair. Now he was as lean and as tanned as Californian fitness programmes and sun could make him and his hair was beginning to thin and go grey at the temples. He was good-looking, worldly and conceited—she could tell that from the way he lounged laconically on top of the beclothes with his pyjama jacket casually hanging open beneath his loosely tied silk dressing-gown so that everyone could catch a glimpse of his bronzed pectorals. It annoyed her. In the past she had sometimes dreamed of Tony returning to her, showering her with the love she had missed so much. And then she had met Giles and begun to realise for the first time what an adult, responsible relationship might bring; how much more lasting and deep the love. Seeing Tony at last, she felt the last shreds of her interest in him evaporate. Fifteen years ago his style and panache might have impressed her, but now she knew that she would risk everything for a man with an egg-stain on his lapel or a nick in his chin. In fact she *had* risked everything for him . . . And look where it had got her.

'Why didn't you let us know you were coming over? I'm sure Dan would have loved to have seen you.' Her question was sharp, defensive, and Tony's eyes narrowed in peeved surprise

'I was only supposed to be here a couple of days and I didn't want to have to make any promises to Dan if I wasn't going to be able to keep them,' he shrugged casually. 'Anyway, he's not exactly my son, is he?'

'He certainly is! I don't know what you're suggesting . . .' Louise's voice rose sharply.

'I don't mean biology! But he's grown up with you and he scarcely knows me from Adam. When he came over to New York I heard nothing but stories about you. How Mum had done this and Mum had been promoted and he and Mum . . . What I mean is that you're a damn hard act to follow. We were like strangers; friendly strangers. It's not your fault, I know. I didn't try to keep up with the boy,' he added hastily, seeing an unfamiliar fighting gleam deepening Louise's eye. 'Anyway, I thought perhaps it was best if I didn't make a big fuss about coming over here.'

'Thanks for your honesty.' Louise, half-surprised at the ease with which he had admitted he

was in the wrong, busied herself pouring him some
orange juice. Tony watched her avidly, discovering
anew the woman he'd once married. It was a shock
to realise how much she had changed, how inde-
pendent she was. Even when he had left her he had
carried her with him as a sort of impossible ideal
which no other woman could hope to live up to.
They had been very close, shared hopes and
dreams which he had never shared with anyone
since. If they had been older—if he had been
older—they might have worked their way through
their troubles and escaped divorce. But he had
been a young fool, wanting everything at once . . .
Sometimes on his holidays he found himself scan-
ning the beach for Louise, praying that an impossible
coincidence might happen and that she and Dan
might be some miracle have flown to Hawaii or
Barbados. Often he'd found himself wondering
what she was doing. But he'd never done anything
about it, never had the courage to invite her to New
York to admire his new life. And now here she was,
and every inch of her neat figure and firm gestures
told him that she didn't want to know him.

'We had some good times together, didn't we,'
he said quietly, taking the glass from her. 'Do you
ever look back on those days and think they were
the best?'

'Only when I'm depressed. Looking back makes
me feel much happier about the present.' Quite
where her rudeness came from, Louise didn't
know. But she did know that she wasn't going to
pretend; those days had been good but not,
obviously, good enough. Tony had brushed off his
responsibilities and left her with them. She was not
going to let him forget that. He wasn't going to get

away with just pretending it was some sort of joke.

'I hadn't realised that you were so bitter,' he said with a mocking edge to his voice that concealed the wound she had given him with that final putdown.

'Oh, I'm not bitter,' Louise said lightly. 'Just annoyed that you seem to come and go just as you please, forgetting us when it's convenient and then talking about what good times we had together when we do finally meet. You have a very short memory.'

The stabbing pain of guilt that he had carried with him for all these years silenced Tony's retort. Yes, he'd always realised how badly he'd behaved; yes, he knew that Louise must have had a hard time; but no, he had never quite got around to doing anything about it, checking up on her. He had no right to forgiveness. Still, she was very attractive and, despite the years and all that had happened he still felt the chemistry that had drawn them to each other in the first place. Perhaps, given some time to get used to his presence, she would relax, begin to understand him better. He'd never met a woman who could make him feel the way she did. With a little luck, who knew. Maybe they could rediscover what they had once shared.

Louise looked over the bedtable at the huge bowl of fruit, the box of chocolates, the tissues, the flowers and cards, all from his friends and admirers at the film studios. 'Is there anything you want?' she asked doubtfully.

'No, nothing.' He allowed a tinge of regret to creep into his voice. He watched as Louise got to her feet, smoothed her skirt and pulled on her heavy winter coat.

'I'll come in and see you when I can. I'll send Dan

SISTER SLATER'S SECRET   179

along too. Now you're here he might as well visit you,' she added frostily. 'You're in very good hands. Mr Levete is an excellent surgeon.'

'I'm sure he is. And I gather that he has been a very good friend to you.' Tony's eyes caught the momentary flush that warmed her cheeks.

'If you have started to believe hospital gossip then I'm afraid there's no hope for you,' Louise snapped. 'You've only been here six hours; wait until you've had a day or two of it and then you'll know not to believe a thing you're told.' Picking up her handbag she left him lying, startled, on the bed.

The wind whipped around her ankles as she walked down the hospital drive and stung her cheeks with such ferocity that she didn't realise for a few moments that she was crying. Today she had laid Tony's ghost to rest. Today Giles had made it perfectly clear that there was to be no future with him. She was on her own again, and this time it was for always. Reaching the main road, she made a split-second decision. She would not go straight home. Tonight she would go into the centre of the city and do some late-night shopping. Christmas was only a few weeks away and she had done nothing to prepare for it. In the bustle and the crush of the late-night shoppers she could lose herself, become anonymous—and forget for just a few hours that there was no man waiting for her to come home . . .

'Tell me, is Louise Slater always as frosty as she was with me this afternoon?' Tony lay back on the bed while Giles performed yet another examination, listening attentively to the man's heartbeat.

'She has a reputation of being very efficient and

cool,' Giles admitted in an absent-minded tone that belied the fact that every inch of his tall figure was straining for some news of Louise and her reaction to the sudden appearance of her ex-husband.

'You know that we were married?' Tony asked casually.

'Yes, I do.' Giles straightened and indicated that Tony could button his pyjama jacket.

The patient watched the surgeon shrewdly—and Giles knew it. Perhaps Tony had guessed that he and Louise were rather more than just friends. Louise would certainly never have told him, surely . . .

'Well, I warn you now that as soon as I'm up and about again I intend to have a go at winning her back again,' Tony said jokingly. Giles went a little pale and his heart began to bump betrayingly in his chest at the news he had feared hearing.

'Just wait until we've got the operation sorted out, will you?' he smiled as lightly as he could. 'You don't need any more excitement at the moment.' Inwardly his mind raced. If he was to stake his claim, try to repair the damage he had done in the past few days, he must act now, before Tony could leap in and catch Louise on the rebound.

'I'll see you tomorrow morning, Mr Slater,' he said eagerly. 'Sister will give you something to make you sleep comfortably. I've told you all I can about the operation, but if you have any more questions about what we'll be doing, please let one of the staff know and I'll make sure I come and answer them.'

Tony waved him airily away and picked up the lurid paperback he'd been given to read—one which was perhaps not the best choice for a man

with heart problems. Giles sped from the ward as if
pursued by demons. He must find Louise quickly;
he knew now what he had to do, whatever the
problems and the practicalities. Please God he
wasn't too late and she hadn't begun to warm to the
man who had returned so unexpectedly after all
these years!

'Oh—it's you.' Dan hesitated in the hallway, un-
certain whether to slam the door in Giles's face or
to invite him in. Illuminated by the porch light
Giles looked huge and forbidding, just as he had
the night he'd dragged Becca from the house.
'Mum's not in. I expect she's gone shopping,' Dan
explained, licking his lips which had suddenly gone
dry with nervous tension.

'Can I come in and wait?' Giles felt the discomfort too. He had behaved badly, not just here the
other night but afterwards, to Dan and to Louise. 'I
promise I won't cause any scenes. In fact I'd like to
sit down and have a good chat with you. I think
there are some things you ought to know.'

'I don't know . . .' Dan's distrust was not easily
overcome. 'I don't know how long she'll be, you
see.'

The impasse was resolved by Cosmo, who came
tearing up the garden path and placed himself
nonchalantly at Giles's feet, purring like a well-
conditioned lawn-mower. Giles bent down to
stroke the cat, then gently picked him up and
rocked him like a baby. 'Let me bring him in. I
won't outstay my welcome—not if you will make
me welcome.'

'All right. You can come in and I'll make some
tea. I was going to have a bacon sandwich. You can

have one if you want.' Still on his guard, Dan led the way into the house.

'Do you mind if I use your phone?' The sight of it in the hallway had given Giles a bright idea.

'So long as you don't call Australia,' Dan muttered grimly. This man had a damned cheek. And yet perhaps he wasn't so bad; after all, his mother had been terribly upset when he'd stormed off with Becca, and she'd been very quiet ever since.

'I'm going to call Becca and ask her to come round here, if you don't mind. And here's something to cover the call.' With a glint of amusement in his eye, Giles offered the boy ten pence. In a perverse way he rather liked the lad's grudging attitude. At least it showed a bit of spirit, and he wasn't actually being rude.

'If you're really going to call Becca you can do it for free.' Dan's eyes lit up with eagerness. 'And ask her if she wants a bacon sandwich, will you? I can have it ready by the time she arrives.'

'Will do.' With a wry laugh Giles lifted the receiver. What he was about to do was quite beyond reason. It was the mark of a man quite incapable of controlling his emotions. But he wanted Louise, and the only way he was going to get her was to risk everything he had; to fill his life with problems and responsibilities—and love. With a determined finger he dialled the number and Dan, unable to believe that this was really happening, went through to the kitchen to lay the bacon on the grill and switch on the kettle.

An hour later and the three of them were still sitting around the table in the kitchen, Dan and Becca kept a reasonable distance from each other as they concluded their business. Empty plates and mugs had been pushed to one side and Giles was busily writing something on a sheet of paper, which was already almost covered with various resolutions and motions.

'I think that's it, unless either of you have ideas you'd like to include,' Giles said finally as he put down the pen.

'We've got equal rights for Dan and me, haven't we?' Becca checked. 'I don't want to find that I'm landed with all the cooking and cleaning while he goes off to his Saturday job.'

'It's in paragraph three,' Giles sighed wearily. 'I suppose you can have a Saturday job if you really want one, Becca, though there's no need for you to have one. You get plenty of pocket money.'

Dan and Becca exchanged despairing looks. 'Of course, Louise hasn't seen this yet, so we may have to alter things or add a few clauses.'

'Does she know about this?' Dan asked curiously. After all, this man had walked in and taken over the kitchen, insisting that they all sit down and draw up a contract by which they could all live as a family—and he didn't even seemed to have consulted the woman he wanted to marry about it!

'No, she doesn't—but I hope it will be a lovely surprise.' Giles handed Dan the pen. 'Here you are, just sign here. You've read the small print?'

'Yes.' Dan raised a bemused eyebrow at Becca, who was gazing skywards as if she couldn't believe what was happening. 'No hanky-panky or we get sent off to school . . . What about the holidays? There's plenty of time to get up to mischief then!' His eyes danced with laughter.

'You will go to your relatives for school holidays, if necessary, and Becca will go to stay with her grandmother in Kircudbrightshire.' Giles grinned broadly. 'And if that fails, I can always send you rock climbing or canoeing in one of the more isolated bits of the country each summer.'

'Fair enough.' Dan shrugged. If the truth were known, he'd been quite relieved when Giles had broken up the engagement celebration he had planned. Deep down he was a sensible lad; he knew it would be folly to get too involved with Becca, who was being pursued by every boy at school. He'd seen how she flirted with Benvolio in the play and spent her time off-stage making eyes at Tibalt. She was young and flighty, he'd told himself, and he didn't really want to get tied down . . . He scrawled his signature, still rather large and schoolboyish, at the bottom of the page. Becca took the pen and paper and did likewise and Giles followed.

'Now, one last thing,' he announced. 'Have you still got that engagement ring anywhere, Dan? I'll take it off you for whatever you paid for it.'

'What do you want it for?' Becca asked, amazed.

'I don't normally carry one about on me, silly, and if I'm to do this properly I need all the equipment—like an engagement ring,' Giles explained patiently.

The sudden relief of making the decision to propose had gone to his head like wine; he would not rest happily until he had asked Louise to marry him. Between them, he, Becca and Dan had come to an arrangement, an agreement for how they could live together. That had been surprisingly easy, for both children had seemed delighted at the prospect of living in a proper family again. Now came the difficult bit. After all he had done and said, could he seriously expect Louise to accept him? He buried his head in his hands for a few moments. Dan rose from the table and went up-stairs and Becca began diplomatically clearing away the plates and mugs.

Would she say yes? With Tony now on the scene? Giles ran his long-fingered hand through his hair, then brushed the stubble on his cheek. He needed a shave; it was late in the day and his beard grew quickly. How could he propose to Louise without a shave first? Tony Slater, dapper and compact, would never have been caught out like this.

'Here you are.' Dan put the little jewellers box down on the table. Giles opened it. The ring glittered quite impressively. Maybe it wasn't worth a fortune—it was quite good enough for the purpose.

'I'll write you a cheque,' Giles said quietly, reaching down to his briefcase.

'I don't have a bank account,' Dan said, embarrassed at the admission. 'Take it now and pay me later, if she accepts. And by the way, if she accepts, what do I call you?'

'And what do I call her?' Becca asked. 'Mum?'

'Whatever pleases you,' Giles sighed wistfully. 'Of course, we may have done all this for nothing.' He slipped the tiny box into his pocket. 'I don't think I can propose with you two here. We'll have to go somewhere.'

'Out on the heath, in the dark. It's very romantic,' Becca advised, wiping down the table.

'It's also very cold. But I don't think I really want to go to a restaurant,' Giles admitted. 'So maybe, if we wrap up warmly, the heath would be the spot.'

*   *   *

'Okay, you've got me here, in the freezing cold and pitch dark. Now say what you have to say and let me go home!' Louise had arrived home to find Giles waiting for her and Becca and Dan giggling in the background. She was cold and tired and felt emotionally exhausted after the end of a very trying day—and then all three of them had implored her to go for a walk on the heath with Giles.

Hadn't he played around with her enough? Hadn't he led her on, despite all her defences, made her make a fool of herself, and then promptly told her that it was no use crying over spilt milk —that there could be nothing between them? Why, only this morning he had demanded a professional relationship with her and nothing more . . . But one look at that tall, lean, strong-shouldered figure, his manly beard beginning to show through dark under the skin, and her resolve to forget him had vanished, even though her short temper had not. And the warmth and weight of his arm around her shoulders as he led her on to the heath was not enough to dispel her frustration with him.

The lights of the whole of north London seemed to twinkle around them as they picked their way along one of the paths that criss-crossed the heath. The wind had dropped, but it was still cold and gusty. Louise pulled herself into Giles's side, forgetting all the harsh words that had been said. To be here with him was bliss, however short-lived the peace. If she were to forget him, escape from him, then she would have to move and change jobs. Because while he was around her heart could never be her own. He'd taken it from her and he still had it, no matter how much she wanted it back. A kind word, a smile—she would be forever betraying herself, as she was tonight.

Giles drew her off the path and into a little culvert, complete with bench, that was slightly sheltered from the wind. He brushed a dried leaf from the seat and motioned Louise to sit.

'We've got to have a serious talk, you and I,' he began, and the nervousness in his voice made her wonder.

'As you told me this morning, we have nothing to discuss . . .' she started, only to be silenced by a kiss as his mouth came down fairly and squarely on hers.

'Do you love Tony?' The question, on top of the kiss, surprised her into silence. Giles's breath hung heavily in the quiet night. 'Do you?' he urged, taking her hand almost unconsciously and stroking it between his own strong fingers.

'No, of course I don't, but what's that to do with . . .' This time Louise saw the kiss coming and leaned into him to meet it. She didn't know why she was here or what his plans were, but his kiss she could not deny herself, come what may. Their lips lingered this time, and Giles's fingers came up to cradle her head to his chest.

'Marry me, then.' His voice was harsh with emotion and feeling he'd thought he'd never know again, not after their last parting. 'I've even got an engagement ring to prove to you that I'm serious.' From his pocket he brought Dan's little box and Louise laughed aloud when she saw it.

'Is this your idea of a joke, Giles Levete? You bring me out here in Arctic temperatures and offer me an engagement ring you've borrowed from my son?'

'I've never been more sincere about anything in my life!' Giles laughed too, scarcely able to believe what was happening. 'You're supposed to say yes, you know, otherwise all my plans have been wasted.'

'What plans are these?' Louise wanted to believe him, wanted to say yes and hold him in her arms, but having been denied her happiness for so long she felt she couldn't tell him that she longed to. 'Are you planning a ten-year engagement, perhaps? Is your idea that we get married when the children reach the age of thirty and can be responsible for themselves?' she mocked. 'Or some sort of arrangement that will have the Sunday papers on the doorstep in no time . . . You living in one house with Becca and me in the other with Dan?' The gleam of his eyes in the darkness made her pause. Could she put up with a long engagement? or living apart from him? Yes, her heart replied. Yes, if it meant that some day they could be together. 'Tell me,' she said quietly.

'I've come to an agreement with Dan and Becca. We've made a contract and I've decided to trust them.' He faltered. 'You've taught me to trust them, to trust the world again, Louise. You didn't know it, but there have been times when I've wanted to hurt everyone I've met, to stop them hurting me—or Becca. I began to realise that if someone who had been as badly hurt as you could be trust *me* then I would have to return that trust. It's difficult when you've been through what we've been through . . .'

'I know.' Louise's lips sought out his cheek, then his mouth and they kissed for a long time in the darkness.

'There was no need to propose, though. I don't love Tony and I've no intention of marrying anyone else . . . Surely you know that I love you?' Her voice was a whisper. 'And if you really think it will be a disaster if we all try to live as a family . . . I'll trust you; I'll wait; I'll do anything you want me to do.' He held her so close that she could feel his heart beating under his jacket and the hardness of his ribs.

'I want to marry you and have you for my wife. It is as simple as that. And why I didn't say so a month ago I don't know. I'm a fool.'

'And what about Dan and Becca? You don't still want to send Becca away to school, do you? It would be the worst thing you could do.' Louise paused. 'In fact if that's your plan, I won't marry you. I won't make her unhappy . . .'

'Be quiet and let me talk!' Giles's fingers traced her lips, her jaw, ran down her throat and round and up into her hair. 'The children and I have drawn up a contract with rules on how we will all get along together. I'm not allowed to make decisions about what time they go to bed and whether they take Saturday jobs, but in return they have agreed to inform us of where they're going and with whom and what time they're coming home. They've also agreed to behave themselves . . .' he kissed her softly again . . . 'on the understanding that if they still feel strongly for each other when Becca's eighteen they can do what they like. I know Becca would dearly love to have a woman at home again, and she thinks you're terrific, so that may have swayed things.'

'But what happens if anyone breaks the contract? There'll be dreadful rows . . . It's a nice idea but not a very practical one,' Louise sighed, pulling away. 'You can't run lives by contracts. Even the legal profession have problems. Tear it up and I'll marry you and we'll just have to cope as best we can.'

Giles took the sheet of paper out of his pocket. 'You don't think it will work?' he asked cautiously.

'We'd have to have it framed and hung in the hall, and if there was an argument we'd have to go through it looking for loopholes . . . No, it wouldn't work. But trust and love will. Dan and Becca aren't stupid. They know in their hearts that what they've been up to doesn't lead to happiness. They've got two classic examples in front of them, haven't they?'

'Not any more they haven't. We're going to be the happiest couple in the whole world,' Giles growled, 'and that might just encourage them to copy us . . .'

'Yes, I'll marry you.' Louise's words vanished as he kissed her again and again. At last they had to come up for air.

'What about Tony?' Louise murmured, warm and happier than she'd ever been before, now that she had the comfort and security of his arms. 'Won't it be difficult for you to operate on him tomorrow, knowing that we were once married?'

'Not at all,' Giles laughed. 'It's all the more incentive for me to do a good job and get him up and out of the country as soon as possible. Though perhaps it might be diplomatic for us to keep quiet about this engagement until he's gone. The strain could be very bad for him. Would you mind waiting a while before it becomes public?'

Louise's kiss assured him that she wouldn't.

'Let's get back to the kids,' she said at last. 'Goodness knows what they're up to.'

As they pulled up in the car the front door opened wide and two flushed faces greeted their parents.

'Well,' Becca asked as Louise preceded Giles up the path, 'did you say yes?'

'Yes. I'm going to enjoy having a daughter after all these years,' Louise greeted her—and then they were in each other's arms and Becca was hugging her for all she was worth.

'And I'm going to love having you for a new Mum . . .' The words made Louise's heart, already full to overflowing with happiness, glow even more warmly.

'Hello, Dad.' Dan's greeting was more restrained, but out of the corner of her eye Louise thought she saw a tear on his cheek. 'And don't forget that you owe me for the engagement ring.'

Giles cast an amused look in Louise's direction and shrugged. 'As I suspected,' he smiled, 'all our troubles are only just about to begin—and I'm going to love every single one of them!'

Doctor Nurse Romances

Amongst the intense emotional pressures of modern medical life, doctors and nurses often find romance. Read about their lives and loves in the other two Doctor Nurse titles available this month.

FLYING DOCTOR
Lilian Darcy

Working for the Australian Royal Flying Doctor Service was an exciting new challenge for Janet Green. Unfortunately the senior doctor at the Base, Clifford Ransome, was convinced that she would soon rush back to the city nursing heat exhaustion and a broken heart. How could she convince him that she really cared about her work in this savagely beautiful outback?

NO CURE FOR LOVE
Leonie Craig

'I seem to be upsetting Sister, and we can't have that, can we!' Lucas Mallory commented sarcastically after crossing swords with Sister Jo Blake. Jo had returned from sick leave to find the devastatingly attractive new consultant neurologist had completely disrupted her orderly routine — she wasn't going to let him disrupt her nervous system as well!

Mills & Boon
the rose of romance